Calypso

A Harry Starke Novel

By

Blair Howard

Calypso
Copyright © 2016 Blair Howard

ISBN-13: 978-1539190059

Cover design: Tim Brenner
Website: https://tpkbrenner.wordpress.com/

Calypso – A Harry Starke Novel

"The most loving parents and relatives commit murder with smiles on their faces."—*Jim Morrison*

"There are four basic reasons why someone commits murder. The first and most powerful is love. The second—equally powerful—is hate. Almost equally compelling is revenge. The fourth is profit. Money. When one family member kills another, one or more of them is almost always the motive, and the murders on Calypso Key were no exception."—*Harry Starke*

It was one of those beautiful, balmy days on Calypso Key in the US Virgin Islands. The sky was blue and a cool breeze was blowing in off the ocean as Harry and Amanda took their vows. All of their friends were there and all was well with the world... and then the sky fell.

Harry draws the line at getting involved when the death of one of his father's friends intrudes upon his wedding day—until he finds out he owes the girl's father a debt he can never repay. And so he is dragged into an investigation of not just one murder, but two—and the wealthiest, most dysfunctional family he's ever met. The cast of characters includes a former Navy Seal turned butler, a man up to his eyes in shady financial dealings, and the woman at the heart of it all, who was pushed to her death from a third-story balcony. Harry clears a few hours to enjoy the good life on Calypso Key, but as for the investigation... well, we all know that when Harry's involved, nothing is ever quite what it seems.

Chapter 1

"Dearly beloved, we are gathered together here in the sight of God, and in the face of this company, to join together this man and this woman in holy matrimony, which is commended to be honorable among all men, and therefore...."

Oh my God. Am I really doing this?

Was I having second thoughts? No. I was simply overcome with wonder at what was happing to me. There I was—I'm Harry Starke, by the way—after almost forty-six years as a confirmed bachelor, standing beside one of the most beautiful women I'd ever met, on a sun-drenched island in the Caribbean, taking vows to forever bind me to her. I have to tell you: over the years I'd been through some crazy experiences, most of them good, some of them really bad, but this....

"This occasion marks the celebration of love and commitment with which this man and this woman begin their life together. And now, through me...."

It was just after sunrise. A cool breeze was blowing in off the ocean, over the beach where we stood. I looked around. Everyone was there— my family, my friends; everyone who was important to me. It wasn't a big group. In fact, as wedding parties go, it was kinda small; just twenty-seven people. *Nice, that.*

Yes, my mind was beginning to wander, but I was soon brought back to the moment by a discreet elbow from Bob Ryan, my best man. I closed my eyes, squeezed Amanda's hand, and relished the gentle pressure I felt in return. I turned and looked at her; she smiled up at me; I nodded and smiled back at her.

The minister went on for a few more minutes, and then suddenly I heard:

"Do you, Harry…."

And yes, I did, and so did Amanda, and five minutes later we were in each other's arms and the little crowd was cheering wildly.

What happened next had to be seen to be believed. Bob Ryan grabbed me around the waist, actually hoisted me into the air, and ran with me into the ocean—and as soon as he'd dumped me in he went after Amanda. She tried to run, shrieking, laughing, but it was no good. As big as he is, the man moves like a gazelle, and a minute later he'd dumped her in the water at my side, and then damn it if he didn't take off after Kate. It was the beginning of what promised to be a glorious day. I grabbed Amanda, ignoring the shooting pains in my left arm—from a still-healing gunshot wound; long story—and hoisted her over my shoulder, kicking and yelling and laughing. I headed out with her, away from the beach into deeper water. Hell, I even saw my old man and

2

Rose get into the water…. The only shadow over the proceedings was that my kid brother Hank wasn't there. His death at the hands of one Shady Tree only six weeks before—part of the long story that ended in me getting shot—had hit me and my family hard. But, as they say, life goes on, and I know he would have wanted us all to be happy.

The good times continued on through a very wet lunch—and by wet, I don't mean water—and then into the afternoon, until at last I insisted on being alone, at least for an hour or two, with my new wife.

We were on Calypso Key in the Virgin Islands. I'd booked what could only be called a resort within a resort: a small, private, ocean-side complex of four villas, each with four bedrooms, and a small private cottage, which was where Amanda and I retreated to. The five units came with a small clubhouse, a private bar, a dining room, an infinity pool, and a whole passel of staff that included housekeepers, a chef, full-time bar staff, and… two butlers. That's right, there were two of 'em, and I'd booked it all for two whole weeks. No, you don't wanna know what that was costing me… well, maybe you do, but you're not going to. Ah. Whatever. It was worth it.

Amanda and I had been a couple for almost three years before I'd finally asked her to tie the knot. We'd lived together in my home on Lookout Mountain for almost a year before that, so we were well used to one another. But somehow, that afternoon on Calypso Key, I started to see Amanda in a totally different light. She was as beautiful as ever, but in a very different way. I can't describe it. She had an air about her; it was an almost ethereal thing.

Once we got into the cottage Amanda closed the door, locked it, took my hand, and led me to a place that was probably as close to Heaven as I'm ever likely to get.

It was almost five o'clock that afternoon when we were dragged back to the real world by an insistent banging at the cottage door.

What the hell? I crawled off the bed, wrapped a sheet around me, and headed down the stairs.

I opened the front door and was greeted by two men, one big and black, one tall, skinny, and with much lighter skin. I didn't have to look at them twice to know they were cops. "Mr. Starke? Mr. Harry Starke?" the first one asked.

I looked at them hard. Neither one of them flinched. They both looked me right in the eye.

"Nope," I said, pushing the door closed.

The second one put out a hand and caught it.

"Oh yeah. Pull the other one, Harry," he said, smiling a big, toothy grin. "Yeah, I know it's been a long time, but come on...."

What the hell?

4

It was the grin that did it. I hadn't seen it in more than fifteen years, since I was a rookie cop back in Chattanooga.

"Tommy? Tommy... Quinn? What the hell are you doing here?"

He nodded, still grinning. "It's Lieutenant Quinn now. I'm with the USVI Police Department, Major Crimes Unit on St. Thomas. Oh, and congratulations, by the way. Um... can we come in?"

"No! *Hell* no! I'm all but naked, for one, and two, I just got married. It's nice to see you Tommy, I mean it, but come back another day. We're here for two weeks." Again, I tried to push the door closed. Again, he held it open.

"Yeah, I see the naked thing," he said, grinning, "and I know about you getting married—and I wouldn't be here if I had a choice, but this is official. So c'mon, Harry. Let us in."

"Harry," Amanda called, "whoever it is, tell them we'll meet them at the bar in a couple of hours."

"Now see what you've done," I said. "She was asleep."

"Sorry, Harry, but this is important. We need to talk. We really do."

I sighed, shook my head, and opened the door wide enough for them to enter.

"Two minutes. No more. I mean it, Tommy. I've waited a lot of years for this and I don't want it screwed up."

He nodded. They came in, and the skinny guy closed the door.

"It's the police," I shouted up the stairs. "I'll be up in a few minutes, okay? You don't have to come down."

"The *police*? What is going *on*?" And down the stairs she came, wrapped in a white terrycloth robe. "I *said*, what is going *on*?"

"Honey. This is Lieutenant Tommy Quinn. I know him from way back. And this is…?" I was talking to Quinn, but I was looking at the tall guy, who was standing in the kitchen grinning at Amanda.

"Detective Isaac Rawlson," Quinn said. "Say hello to Harry and Mrs. Starke."

Oh. I almost grinned. *Mrs. Starke. That's a first.*

The detective stuck out his hand toward Amanda. "Pleased t'meet you, ma'am."

She wrinkled her nose and slowly held out her hand, holding her robe closed at the neck with the other.

"You too, I think," she replied.

"Look, Tommy," I said. "I appreciate the visit, but we got married less than six hours ago. So come on. Tell me what you want, and then get outa here."

6

"Can we sit?"

"Hell no we can't sit. Tell me what you want and then go. Hell, Tommy, you can even come back this evening and join us for a drink if you want. Bring... whatever this guy's name is with you. If not, I'll—that is, we'll—meet you both for a drink in a couple of days."

"Harry," Quinn said finally. "Do you know who Leopold Martan is?"

"Martan... no, I don't think... so. Wait a minute, do you mean the industrialist?"

Quinn nodded.

"Not really. He's a friend of my father's. He's in pharmaceuticals, owns Gentech Biomedic, but that's about all I know." My father had defended his company in a lawsuit some ten or twelve years ago, but I'd never even met the guy. "Why do you want to know?"

"There's been a death, Harry. Martan knows you're here and he's asked for—well, he's *insisting* that you be brought in. The chief's having a goddamn fit, but the man wields a big stick around here. He owns most of the real estate on the island, including this resort, and he donates a lot of money to a lot of good causes so... he usually gets what he wants."

"Okay. So what does he—"

"Harry, no," Amanda said. "It's our wedding day, for God's sake." She turned angrily to Quinn. "Go away."

Quinn looked at me helplessly.

I heaved a huge sigh. "I'll listen, but that's all—"

"Ugh!" Amanda whirled and stomped up the stairs.

Well, okay. But what was I supposed to do? "Tommy," I said, "by God this had better be good."

It was good. Well, no—it was bad. Very bad. Martan's twenty-four-year-old daughter had been found on the rocks, dead, forty feet below her bedroom window less than three hours earlier. Quinn and his partner had been called in and had arrived on the island via helicopter less than an hour ago.

"I told Martan I thought it was either an accident or… suicide?" Quinn screwed up his face.

I didn't answer. I stared at him. I knew what was coming.

"The old man's having none of it. He's insisting she was murdered and that you…." He trailed off when he saw me shaking my head. "Yeah," he sighed, getting to his feet. "I can't say as I blame you, but I promised I'd ask. Sorry for the intrusion. Maybe I'll take you up on that drink a little later."

Except then there was another knock on my front door, and once again that sixth sense of mine kicked in and the bottom dropped out of my stomach.

Oh hell, here they are.

And they were. I opened the front door and my father, August, walked in, followed by a man who could only have been Leo Martan.

He was of medium build, maybe five foot ten. His white hair and aquiline features reminded me of those busts you see of Julius Caesar.

"Harry," August said, glancing at Quinn and the other cop. "I assume you've been apprised of the situation. This is Leo—"

"Stop! Stop *right* there. I know who he is and why you're both here, and you can forget it." I glanced up the stairs. Amanda was standing on the landing, arms folded, listening.

"Dad, this is my wedding day, for Christ's sake. I don't want to do this. I want to spend time with Amanda, and with you, with the people I love. I've spent my life working one murder after another. Give me a f... give me a break, will you, please?"

"Mr. Starke." It was Martan who spoke. "I understand how you feel, and I respect that, but I have just lost my only daughter and this man—" he waved his hand at Quinn "—is telling me it was suicide, or even an accident, and with respect, I *know* she didn't commit suicide, and the balcony rail is too high for her to simply have fallen over it."

9

I listened to him, all the while shaking my head. I looked at my father. He stared back at me, and I knew what he was thinking.

"Mr. Starke," Martan said. "She's still out there, on the rocks. I wouldn't let them move her until you'd seen her. All I ask is that you take a look; tell this man it was not suicide. An hour, two at the most. Please."

"Go on, Harry." I hadn't heard Amanda come back down the stairs. "The man needs help. We have two weeks. Two hours won't hurt, and you'll be back here in time for dinner."

"Nope. This time I draw the line. I made you a promise, Amanda, and I intend to keep it. I'm sorry, Mr. Martan, but—"

"Harry," August said. "Do it for me. I owe this man, and even though you don't know it, so do you."

"*What*? What the hell are you talking about? I've never met him before in my life."

"But I have, and so did your mother. In fact, he's responsible for her living as long as she did. You do owe him. We both do. Now go take a look, for God's sake. Amanda's said she doesn't mind."

I looked at her, and she lifted her chin toward the door. "Go on. I'll still be here when you get back."

And that's how it all began. Reluctantly, I climbed the stairs, splashed water on my face, and dressed in a pair of lightweight linen pants and a sports shirt.

"Okay," I said, once I'd come downstairs again. "A quick look. And that is *it*." And then I walked quickly to the front door and out into the afternoon sunshine.

Chapter 2

The ride out only took a few minutes: a mile along the main road, then a sharp right through the electronic gates, and up the hill to the massive structure that the Martans called home. We're talking three stories and maybe fifteen bedrooms. It would, in another time, have been a fortress.

The view to the right of the winding driveway, of the south side of the island and the ocean, was breathtaking. The great house stood on a natural rock formation, almost like a medieval motte, that fell away from the foundations in a gentle slope for maybe four or five hundred feet to a pristine golf course, which circled around the edge of the property.

We were no more than halfway to the house when I spotted the square white tent on the rocks below, several uniforms and Tyvek-covered techs working around it. There was also a private helicopter parked at the rear.

"Looks like you have some help anyway, Tommy," I said. It looked like this would indeed be a short visit; I would soon be on my way back to Amanda.

"They arrived from St. Thomas not long after we did. Harry, I'm really pleased you've agreed to... okay, okay, I know how you feel, but let me say this. It *was* either a suicide or an

12

accident. There's no doubt in my mind. Other than the damage caused by the impact, she's clean; there's not a mark on her that I could see. You'll see."

I nodded, and turned to stare up at the huge home. It was a modern structure: lots of glass and concrete. The south side had been designed to take full advantage of the spectacular view—three stories, four balconies, two over two over a ground-floor patio that stretched the entire length of the south side. The top right balcony, the one nearest us as we approached the house, appeared to be the one from which Gabrielle Martan had taken her final flight.

Quinn parked the car in front of the house, the Range Rover carrying Leo Martan and my father pulling up behind. Together, the five of us walked the short distance to where the techs were working. There was tape up, of course, but no officers standing guard; the property was so isolated that they weren't needed.

"This way," Quinn said as he ducked under the tape.

I followed; Leo Martan and my father stayed outside the perimeter.

"Mind if we suit up?" I asked one of the techs. She shrugged, more or less ignoring me in favor of whatever she was concentrating on. There was a large cardboard box full of one-size-fits-all Tyvek coveralls, and a smaller box full of booties, facemasks, and latex gloves. We donned suits, booties, and gloves.

Inside the tent, a woman of indeterminate age—those coveralls—was on her knees, bent over the body.

"Dr. Jane Matheson?" Quinn said. "This is Mr. Harry Starke."

The woman turned and looked at me, and I could see, even with the mask on, that she was probably in her mid-thirties. She rose, turned, and offered me a latex-covered hand; her grip was strong and sure.

"Mr. Starke," she said. The voice was low, not quite husky. "I know your face already. You've been in the news more than once over the past few years."

I smiled. "Dr. Matheson. Nice to meet you, ma'am. Medical Examiner?"

"Oh no. There's no such thing here on the island. The nearest ME is in St. Thomas. The duties are carried out on a voluntary basis by whoever's available. And right now, that happens to be me."

I frowned inwardly. *Oh boy. A family practitioner.... Not good at all.*

"You don't seem too happy about that," she said dryly.

"Er, no.... That is, no, I'm not *unhappy* about it. It's just not something I'm used to. Our ME back home is a highly experienced

14

pathologist, a forensic scientist. He does all the work; I listen and take notes. With respect, Doctor, this really isn't your field of expertise, is it?"

I could see she was smiling under the mask, obviously not in the least put out by my observation.

"You're absolutely right," she said. "It's not. I'm a gynecologist."

Oh hell. That's even worse.

"But I'll do my best for you."

"Oh, it's not for me. I'm just here as an observer. To give an opinion, if I have one. So, Doctor, how did she die?"

She gave me a slightly incredulous look. "From the fall, of course."

"Do you mind if I take a look?"

"Be my guest."

Gabrielle Martan was lying on her back, legs crossed above the knee, her right cheek lying on her right shoulder. The back of her skull was split wide open and there was a deep cut on her left temple. She was wearing a white bra, panties, and a short, white satin wrap jacket. The outfit wasn't quite transparent, but it left little to the imagination.

I went down on one knee beside her and scanned her quickly from top to bottom to see if anything stuck out, and my heart sank. *Oh shit. Here we go.*

Without getting up, I turned and wiggled my fingers at Matheson. "I need a glass, please."

"Glass? What sort of glass?"

I barely stopped myself from rolling my eyes. "A magnifying glass. You do have one, don't you?"

She didn't.

"It's okay. I'll manage."

I turned back to the body and picked up the girl's left hand. It wasn't stiff, as I'd thought it might be. *Must be due to the warm weather, I suppose.*

I turned her hand palm up. It was clean. Nothing under the nails that I could see. I laid it back on the ground next to her. Her right arm was flung across her chest, and it too was touching the ground. I picked it up: nothing under the nails. I turned it palm down, squinting in the low light. *Oh boy.*

"Tommy. Lift the flap for me please?" He did, and sunlight flooded over the body. I was right. I shook my head and laid her hand back down again.

Next, I leaned in close to examine the wound on her forehead. I sighed, dropped my chin onto my chest, and took a deep breath.

"Okay," I said, rising to my feet. "I have what I need. Let's go see her dad."

He was standing with my father just beyond the tape, and he knew what I was going to say even before I opened my mouth.

"She was murdered, wasn't she?"

I nodded as I stripped off the latex gloves.

"No doubt about it."

Quinn sucked in air, but before he could speak, Jane Matheson said, "You can tell from thirty seconds with the body?" The look she gave me was incredulous.

"The evidence, and the body, speak for themselves. Tommy, you need to get her to a medical center where she can be properly posted by a qualified pathologist, and quickly, before the onset of serious putrefaction. You're also going to need a full tox screen done. What facilities do you have?"

"Not many. The nearest forensic center with a resident pathologist is in Charlotte Amalie, on St. Thomas."

"Then that's where she needs to go. Can you organize a helicopter?"

"Hmmm. There's a Lifeforce unit at the medical center that can carry bodies—our police units aren't fitted out to do it—but…."

"No buts, Tommy. Get on the phone and get them moving, and quickly, before we—before you, I mean—lose what little evidence there is."

"Hang on, Harry, jeez. I gotta call the chief before anything else can happen." He turned

17

away, pulling his phone from his pocket. He talked, and nodded, talked some more, nodded some more, and then hung up.

"It'll be on its way soon. Now, Harry. You wanna tell me and Mr. Martan what's up, or what?"

"Yes, of course. I'm sorry, Mr. Martan, to have made you wait, but it was important that we—you—no, *they*—" I nodded at Quinn and the doctor "—move on this as quickly as possible." I paused for a moment to think about how I was going to handle this.

"There's no doubt in my mind that she was murdered. It was, I think, the fall that killed her. Her skull has suffered a major fracture...." I shook my head. "And she was alive when she hit the rocks. The back of her head is completely crushed. That was caused by the fall...." Again I had to stop to think.

"But the gash on the left side her forehead was not caused by the fall. It's not deep enough, and… well, Doctor, did you notice how the blood from it had run not only down the front of her cheek, but also down the left side of her head and around the top of her ear? This indicates to me that she was either standing or sitting upright when she received the blow to her head. The fact that the blood continued to flow means she was still alive after she received the blow. The blood from the cut ran down past the corner of her left eye. She fell to the floor, unconscious, and for

18

several minutes she must have been on her back, which is when the direction of the blood flow changed and it ran down the side of her head. There'll probably be some of it on the floor, or her bed: somewhere. Someone gave her a hefty bang on the head with a blunt instrument."

Silence. Not a word from any of them, including the doctor, and then Martan asked, "How do you know that?"

I was about to make a joke and say that I watched a lot of television, but that would have been inappropriate, and it wouldn't have been true, either.

"I had a good teacher. Doc Sheddon, the Hamilton County Medical Examiner. Pity he isn't here. I did invite him, but he was too busy to come."

"So that's it?" Matheson said. "Well, personally, I think that cut could well have been caused by the fall—"

"No, it couldn't," I interrupted. "Not unless the poor girl bounced. The contusion was caused by a blow with a blunt instrument. It's V-shaped, maybe the edge of a two by four. There's nothing on the rocks that could have caused such a wound; I looked and, like I told you, it's not deep enough to have been caused by the impact of such a long fall. And there's more. There are bruises on her right wrist—"

19

"What?" Now she interrupted me. "I saw no bruises."

"I know you didn't, which is why I asked you for a glass. But they are there, believe me; very light, barely formed; they were inflicted maybe seconds before her death, but they are very much in evidence. Someone grabbed her by her right wrist and pulled her, probably to either carry or drag her to the window. That too indicates that she was murdered. Doc, I've been around dead people all my adult life. I know what to look for and what it means when I find it. Take my word for it. She was murdered." I turned from her to Quinn.

"Have your techs been through that room yet?"

"I believe so, yes."

"What did they find?"

He was already shaking his head. "Nothing, I think."

"Tell them to go over it again. Don't tell them what they should be looking for. They should know that already. It's there. Believe me; they just have to find it."

"What are they looking for?"

"Blood, medium-impact blood spatter, and the weapon. Come on, Tommy. I know it's remote out here, but hell, you can't have forgotten *everything*. There won't be much. The spatter, the droplets, will be tiny, but they will be there. There may also be some on the floor, or the bed, wherever she lay after being knocked unconscious, but I would expect the killer to have cleaned that up. If so, there may be a wet patch on the carpet, floor, whatever, but Luminol should bring it up. If solvents were used to clean up, you'll need to go over it with phenolphthalein. There will also be some blood spatter on the assailant's clothing, but good luck with that one. You also need to get a real crime scene unit on site."

"It's already here, what we have. Harry, these are the Islands. We're not a big department. We have a small forensics unit that can handle the sort of crime we usually have, and they're here, but, well, you get the idea, right?"

I nodded. St. Thomas was a typical small-community PD. They did a great job of policing the area, but when it came to a major murder investigation…. Well, they just weren't quite as well equipped as most major US cities.

"Okay." I looked at Martan, and my father, and at Quinn. "I took a look. I told you what you needed to know. Now I need to go back to my wife, family, and friends. Tommy. You driving?"

"There's no need for that," Martan said. "I'll take you."

I said goodbye to Matheson and offered her my hand. She took it, reluctantly, gave it a gentle squeeze, and then dropped it.

Okay, so I stepped on your toes. Too bad.

I said goodbye to Quinn and Rawlson and waited while my father climbed into the Range Rover, and then I climbed in after him.

During the short drive back to the resort Martan said not a word, not even thank you or goodbye, and I didn't blame him one bit. What I'd just laid on him had probably devastated him.

He didn't even get out of the car once we arrived. He waited just long enough for me and my father to exit, and then he drove slowly away, staring, unblinking, out through the windshield, his mind obviously elsewhere.

Amanda was poolside, in an open cabana with Kate, Jacque, Rose—and Wendy, Jacque's partner. Bob was nowhere to be seen, and the other members of our party were sitting under umbrellas sipping on a variety of exotic drinks, said drinks being refreshed as needed, or not, by an over-zealous waiter.

Amanda rose to her feet when she spotted me. "Was it…."

"Bad?" I asked, somewhat impatiently. "Yes. It was bad. Was it murder? Yes. It was murder. Now. That's it. Okay? I don't want to talk about it; I just want to forget it, relax, and enjoy the rest of the evening with you."

I said nothing to the rest of the party. Why would I? We'd left the job far behind, back in

Chattanooga. This was downtime, and that was exactly how I wanted it.

To tell the truth, though, I didn't really know how I felt. My emotions were churning. I was angry at being disturbed on my wedding day, sad about what had happened to the girl, and... hell, I was curious, too. What had happened up there on the Mount had all the markings of a case that could have been tailor-made just for me, and I had to admit... I had the itch, and that bothered me even more.

Chapter 3

My bad mood didn't linger long. How could it? I'd just married the girl of my dreams. I was surrounded by all of the people in the world I held dear, and I was on a Caribbean island with a large measure of Laphroaig in my hand, listening to a live steel band playing soft calypso music. Hell, there was even a full moon. How lucky can one man get?

We were outside on the private patio of our resort within a resort, seated for dinner. It was as formal a dinner as it could possibly be considering the situation and location, which meant it wasn't formal at all. We were all dressed for the occasion—shorts, flowered Hawaiian shirts, flip-flops, whatever. I was seated with Amanda at the head of the table. My father and Rose were on my left; Bob, my best man, and Kate Gazzara were on my right.

That little romance was progressing nicely, by the way, but there couldn't have been two more unlikely folks in the world than those two.

We dined on fresh conch salad, peas and rice, salt fish fritters, battered and fried Caribbean lobster, and spiced bread pudding, or "pudín de pan." There was even a small, traditional wedding cake. All of it prepared by our personal chef. Wine, beer, brandy? Oh yes. Plenty of that. And by nine o'clock that evening we were all a little the worse for wear from overeating and over

24

imbibing. And the party got a little noisy, but never rowdy.

After dinner, the pool became the focus of the celebration; everyone but Tim ended up in the water.

I know what you're thinking: skinny dipping, right? Wrong. There was not a bare ass or breast to be seen anywhere. Poor Tim, not usually one to drink, bless him, was asleep on a lounger, his iPad cuddled against his chest, his glasses safe in Sammie's bag, but Sammie, Tim's girlfriend, was hardly in better shape than he was.

Jacque? It was as if she'd come home. Dressed only in a brightly colored halter top and a very short wraparound skirt, she was on the tiny stage with the band, dancing to the toxic rhythm of "Island in the Sun," watched lovingly by her partner, Wendy. Why am I telling you all this? To set the mood, of course. Good times were a happenin'. I was inordinately happy and at peace with the world; Gabrielle Martan was gone from my mind... but not for long.

"Excuse me sir."

I was sitting at a table, poolside, wet and sipping on something red and fruity with rum in it, that tasted like... hell, I have no idea what it tasted like. I know it was good. I looked up to find one of the resort concierges standing behind me.

"Hey. What can I do for you?" I smiled up at him, and then I saw who was with him, and the smile turned into a scowl.

I stood, kicked the chair out of the way, and turned to face Tommy Quinn, Leo Martan, and two men I didn't recognize, both in suits.

The concierge backed away, turned, and walked very quickly from the property. The four men stood their ground. I looked at Quinn. He stared, straight-faced, back at me. He didn't look happy.

I looked at Martan and, as I did so, I was joined by Amanda, my father, and Rose. The band stopped playing, and the entire company froze as if Medusa had suddenly appeared and turned them all to stone.

For a moment, nobody spoke, and then Martan said, his voice so low I could barely hear it, "Mr. Starke…."

"No," I interrupted. "You're disturbing my very special evening. Please leave."

The man looked haggard; his face was drawn, his eyes were watering, and he was twisting his hands together.

"What is it, Leo?" my father asked quietly.

"Dad?"

"Shut the hell up, son. The man's in pain. Can't you see that? The least we can do is listen to him for Christ's sake." He grabbed my upper arm. "Give us a couple of minutes," he told them, then pulled me away out of earshot; Amanda followed.

"What the hell?" I jerked my arm away from him and almost passed out from the pain that speared upward from my still-healing wound.

"Jesus!" I gasped, then took a deep breath. "What the hell, Dad?"

"I'm sorry, but you need to listen to him. We owe him big."

"Okay, so explain. You said he was responsible for Mom living as long as she did, how....?"

"When they diagnosed your mother with cancer, they gave her less than a year to live. It was hopeless. I didn't know what to do. This was back in the early eighties, so there was nothing available, not like there is now. I wasn't the lawyer then that I am today. I'd just defended Leo in a workman's comp case—and won it, but only just. I'd heard there were new drugs coming along, but they were years away from FDA approval. So I turned to Leo. I knew, of course, that he was in pharmaceuticals. He got us the drugs we needed. Thanks to him, your mother lived another three years. You have to listen to him, Harry. It's the right thing to do."

"Harry," Amanda said quietly. "Go back and listen to what they have to say. Please."

"What? What happened to 'Never again, Harry'?" I asked her. "After last time—"

"I know," she said, looking away, then back toward me. Her gaze was steady. "But Harry, you have to."

She was right, and I did. I returned to where Martan and the others were standing, nodded at Martan, and said, "Let's go into the cottage. It's quieter."

I beckoned for Jacque and asked her to get the party going again, telling her we'd be back soon.

As I'd suspected, the two men in suits were both cops—and not just any cops; one was the police commissioner, the other was the chief. Both had flown in by helicopter from St. Thomas. Quinn, we already knew.

Even before they began, I knew where it was going, and I was boiling. Any other time.... *Yeah, but people don't die to a schedule.*

"Okay," I said, once the introductions were done with, "what... what do you want, Mr. Martan?"

"I want you, Harry." He didn't fool around. He came right out with it. "I want you to investigate my daughter's death."

I dropped my chin to my chest, and then brought it up again, slowly shaking my head.

"Why? Tommy here's a good detective. He can do it."

"He may be a good detective, but he's not you." He looked at Tommy. "Lieutenant Quinn, I'm sorry, but you said it was suicide. It wasn't."

I glanced at Tommy. He looked very uncomfortable.

"Harry, I've known your father here for more years than I can remember. I've followed

28

your career with great interest. You are the best there is… no, no. Listen. It's true, and everyone in this room knows it. I know you're in the private practice, if that's the right term for it, and I'm willing to pay whatever you ask—please, let me finish. I will pay whatever you ask. Furthermore, Commissioner Walker and Chief Lawton have agreed to cooperate. Isn't that so, gentlemen?"

I wasn't so sure they had, but they both nodded.

"They have also agreed that Lieutenant Quinn will be made available to work with you, to act as liaison…." And then he ran out of steam, slumped back in his seat, and put his hands over his face. I wasn't sure, but I thought he might have been crying.

I put my hands behind my neck, closed my eyes, and leaned back in my chair. *This is not happening. What the hell did I do to deserve this?*

I looked at my father, then at Amanda. Their faces were like stone. Well, August's was; Amanda's not so much.

For several minutes I just sat there, staring at the wall, thinking: *What the hell? What the hell?*

I looked again at Amanda, shook my head, and shrugged. I just didn't know what to say. I wanted to say no, but… as August had said, we owed the man. I raised my eyebrows at her.

29

"You have to do it, Harry," she said quietly. "It's the right thing to do; you know it is."

She was right. I knew she was, but.... *Hell, it's our* wedding *day.*

I looked at my watch. It was almost nine o'clock and pitch dark outside, but if I was going to do this, it couldn't wait until morning. I had to go right then.

"I need to talk to the others. I can't do this alone. Just give me a couple of minutes. I'll be right back." I rose from my seat and went out to the patio. Bob was back.

I gathered Bob, Jacque, Tim, and Kate together and explained the situation and what I planned to do, and yes, it was my hope that I could rope some if not all of them in: many hands make light work, right?

All I needed Jacque for was to keep track of things, document the investigation: light work that wouldn't take up too much of her and Wendy's time.

Tim I needed for his computer expertise. I'd need background checks done, and maybe more. Kate and Bob.... At that point I had no idea what I was in for. In the initial stage I knew I wanted at least one more pair of eyes and ears—Kate's, if possible—and two would be a blessing. So I filled the four of them in, described my observations up at the Mount, and my analysis, and what I was planning, and then I asked for volunteers.

"Look, I know we're supposed to be on vacation—well, you are; I'm supposed to be on my honeymoon—and I know that it sounds crazy that I'd even consider taking this on. But it's what I... no, it's what *we* do, right? And how long can it take, anyway? Whoever did this has to be a member of the family or an employee. It's a gated property, for God's sake. So, Kate? What about it? Will you lend a hand? Tim?"

"It's your party, Harry," Kate said. "Whatever you ask. You know that."

I've known Kate for more than seventeen years. She was officially my partner when I was a cop, and unofficially from time to time ever since. Except for Amanda, she's my best friend. And I've always been able to count on her.

The other three were nodding, and I felt like... well, I didn't feel good about it.

"You okay with this, Bob?"

Bob's an ex-Chicago PD cop who's been with me almost since the first day I opened the agency. If Kate was my best friend, Bob came in a very tight second. He'd saved my life on more than one occasion, and Amanda's too. So although I could tell he wasn't happy about it, he nodded anyway.

31

"Thanks, Bob," I said. "Jacque, if you and Wendy are okay with it, I'd like you to coordinate everything over the next couple of days."

"Of course. No problem."

"Tim, what equipment do you have with you?"

He grinned at me.

Stupid question.

I smiled back at him and said, "I'll need some background checks done and probably a whole lot of deep digging; is that possible?"

"Yep. The resort has Wi-Fi, so I can connect with my servers back at the office." I stared at him, awed. He grinned, shrugged, looked sheepishly down at the ground, and pushed his glasses up the bridge of his nose with his forefinger. *Geek or not, the boy is a treasure.*

Tim is my IT expert, computer geek, whatever. He's been with me since before he dropped out of college, when he was seventeen and only one small step ahead of the law. Yeah, he was a hacker—still is, when he needs to be. The boy scares the hell out of me sometimes.

"You can do that from here?" I asked. "Everything you can do back at the office you can do here?"

"Pretty much, with a few limitations. The screen on the laptop is kinda small, and—"

"Yeah, yeah, I get it, Tim. That's good, very good." I took a breath. "Kate, how about this: you and I'll go on up there tonight, now, and take a look around the scene, particularly the girl's room. That's where it happened. The rest of you stay here and enjoy what's left of the evening. We'll get together first thing in the morning. Yes?"

They all agreed, and so we had a plan, and Kate and I went back to the cottage, where Amanda, my dad, and the others were still waiting.

"Amanda," I began, "are you absolutely sure you want me to take this on?" She didn't say anything. She simply nodded. I looked at my father, shook my head, and rolled my eyes. He simply stared right back at me, stone-faced. Finally, I turned to face Leo Martan.

"Mr. Martan. This is Lieutenant Catherine Gazzara. She works homicide in the Chattanooga PD Major Crimes unit. She and several others in my party have agreed to help. Here's what I'm prepared to do: I'll do this, but first, Mr. Martan, there's something I need to know you understand. Someone at the house, someone in your family or someone who works for you, killed your daughter. It wasn't an accident. Someone hit her over the head and then threw her off the balcony. That takes a very special type of person, a very dangerous person—a psychopath, maybe even a sociopath."

I looked first at Martan, then at the two police chiefs, then back at Martan. No one spoke.

"Finally…." I stared hard at him. "When I find who did this, I'm turning them over to the police to be prosecuted. That means a member of your family could be charged with capital murder. Do you understand?"

"I do, and I expect no less. How do you intend to proceed? I also need to pay you a retainer…."

"No, sir. There will be no fees."

He opened his mouth to protest, but saw the look I gave him, closed it again, and nodded.

Next I looked at Amanda. She knew what was coming, and she smiled. I'm not sure if she meant it, but she did it anyway, and she nodded.

"Kate and Lieutenant Quinn and I will go to the house now and conduct a survey of both scenes. Tommy, I'll need copies of the crime-scene videos and photographs."

"I need to change first, Harry," Kate said. I nodded. She was wearing a bikini bottom and a T-shirt that had been torn in half, leaving her midriff bare. Not exactly crime-scene attire.

"Ok," I said. "We'll wait." I turned again to Leo. "I'll need a list of everyone who was in the house or on the grounds from eight this morning until now. Everyone, including you and your wife. I want names, Social Security numbers, everything. We'll start conducting interviews tomorrow morning. Do you have a problem with any of that?"

34

"Well no, but my wife, surely you don't…."

"Anyone who was on the property when Gabrielle died is a suspect until we've eliminated them. Including you and your wife, sir."

He nodded. "I understand. I'll draw up the list myself. You'll have it within the hour."

"Just one thing, Mr. Starke," Chief Walker said quietly. "Besides Lieutenant Quinn, how many of my officers will you need?"

I had to think about that for a minute. "I'll need the CSI team, at least for tomorrow morning. I may need to talk to that so-called ME. Can you arrange that?"

He tilted his head slightly. "I'm not sure. She doesn't work for us. I'll have to ask her to call you." He paused, looked at me, and said, "You know, usually, in cases of natural or accidental death, she or Dr. Hayes can do the job. We've never had a murder on Calypso Key. This is new ground for most of us."

"I'm sure," I said. "Where's the body now?"

"At the forensic center in St. Thomas. Dr. Wilson is the senior pathologist."

"I need to get an accurate time of death. Can we call him?"

"I'll do it," Commissioner Walker said. He turned and walked out of the front door, taking his phone from his pocket as he went. He returned a couple of minutes later. "He agreed to do the autopsy first thing in the morning. Do you want to attend?"

"No, I don't think so. I would like to talk to him, though, as soon as he's done. Can that be arranged?"

"Of course. In the meantime, what else do you need?"

"At the moment, nothing. I would like to thank you, though."

"There's no need," Walker said, a little dryly. "Mr. Martan is, well…."

"Yes, of course." I thought I'd save him having to say that Leo was getting preferential treatment because of who and what he was. Politics is, after all, the same the world over. "Now, if you don't mind. We should head up to the house."

Chapter 4

I left Amanda with Rose and my father. Bob wasn't entirely happy about letting Kate leave, but he said he would go for a walk on the beach. Tim and Sammie... well, they were a couple of geeks, and as long as they had their electronics they would be happy wherever they were. The rest of the party would simply hang out and await developments.

The house on the hill was ablaze with lights. We could see the glow of the floodlights almost as soon as we turned onto the road. As we got closer we saw that the white walls were lit up all around the house. There was also a light on in the tent on the rocks below Gabrielle's balcony.

"This is Moore, my butler," Martan said as we reached the top of the steps, and the man waiting for us there. Moore inclined his head, opened the door, and stood aside to let us enter.

The interior of the house was bright and airy. An open, circular foyer gave access to the first-floor living rooms. Two vast staircases—one on either side—swept down from the second-floor landing, which circled the foyer, the doors I saw up there leading, I assumed, to the bedrooms.

"If you would like to see Gabrielle's rooms first," Martan said as we entered the foyer, "Moore will show you the way. In the meantime, I'll get that list for you."

37

"If you'll follow me sir, ma'am," Moore said, leading the way toward the stairs.

Victor Moore looked about as much like a butler as I did. He was wearing an expensive black jacket over a crisp white shirt and black pinstripe trousers, and there the resemblance to Jeeves ended. And then I realized who he reminded me of: this guy and Christopher Walken could have been brothers. Moore was a whole lot younger, maybe in his early forties, but the overall look and demeanor, everything, was the same. This guy's bearing and overall appearance screamed ex-military. And he must have been able to read me, because as soon as we reached the landing he turned and gave me a grin that made my skin crawl; I'd seen friendlier smiles on barracudas. I instinctively looked at the cut of his clothing.

"No, Mr. Starke," he said. The voice was deep, quiet, and smooth, like oil. "I don't have a weapon. I don't need one."

Damn. He read my mind.

"Before we go any further," he said. "I want you to know that I'll do everything I can to help you find the person who killed Miss Gabrielle, and when you do… well, I'll take over from there. She was…. Well, I was her friend, for almost eighteen years, and she was very special to me."

He turned and led the way along the landing to a door that provided access to a second, narrower set of stairs, which led up to the third floor. The techs must have already left for the evening, because the door we stopped at was closed, the frame crisscrossed with yellow tape, and there were a couple boxes of Tyvek covers beside it. *Damn it. I wonder if they found anything.*

"Tommy." I didn't look at him. "I need those techs—well, the one in charge—back here tonight, as soon as possible. Make the call, would you, and ask them to bring whatever records they might have made: videos, photos, diagrams, everything."

"Sure. Her name's Daisy Patel. Patel... petal, Daisy Petal, get it?" The look I gave him would have frozen pump water. "Um, well, okay," he continued, "she's of Indian descent. I'll call her." And he did. "She'll be an hour," he said, holding the phone away from his ear. "Is that okay?"

"She's here on the island, right?"

"Yeah. They're staying at the Windward until we're done with them."

"Good. Then tell her to get up here, now. She doesn't need to dress up for us, and I can't do anything until she gets here. I don't want to disturb the scene until I know she's through with it."

I waited while he talked, then he shut off the phone and pocketed it. "Forty-five minutes. Sooner if she can."

"So," I said, as I turned and headed back toward the stairs. "While we're waiting, we might as well go see if Leo has that list for us."

We found him in his office, a ground-floor room with French windows that overlooked the spot where Gabrielle's body had been found, though the site itself couldn't be seen. The heavy green, yellow, and white-striped curtains had been drawn in front of the windows.

The room was as much a library as it was an office. Floor-to-ceiling bookshelves lined the walls and a vast mahogany desk, flanked by four Chesterfield easy chairs and a sofa, was the centerpiece of a room designed for a man of power and influence. The man himself was seated at the desk, his back to the windows, typing rapidly on a keyboard.

"Ah." He looked up. "That was fast. Come on in. Sit down. I have the list done. I just need to print it. How many copies would you like?"

"A half dozen, if you don't mind—and we're actually not done. We haven't even started. I'm waiting for the crime scene supervisor to arrive."

We sat. He hit a couple keys, stood, walked over to a cupboard, opened the door, and removed a couple dozen sheets of paper from the printer, and handed them to me. There were six sets of four printed pages: names, relationships, birth dates, occupations, socials, and addresses.

"That was quick," I said.

"I'm a methodical man, Mr. Starke. I already had all that information in a computer file. All I had to do was print it. The first two pages contain the family information; the other two pages, the staff."

I handed a copy to Kate and another to Quinn, and then I scanned quickly through the family information.

"This is everyone who was here today, right?" I asked.

"With one exception, yes."

"And that would be…?"

"Gabrielle's fiancé, Sebastian Carriere. He wasn't here on the property. My son Evander… Evan was here in the house. His girlfriend Georgina Walford, my stepdaughter Alicia and her husband Jeffery, they were all here, but they weren't in the house. My eldest son, Leo, was not here; his wife, Lucy, was."

I continued to stare at the list; there were twelve names in all, including his own.

"Sebastian… what? How do you say that again?" I asked.

"Carriere."

I nodded, and repeated it.

41

"Okay, so we have him, but he wasn't here. Let me quickly run down the list and make notes as to who was here and who was not." I looked up at him; he nodded again.

"You and Mrs. Martan, Vivien, were both here, in the house?"

"Yes, all day."

"Your son, Leo Jr., was not here but his wife was?"

"Yes."

"And your son, Evander—Evan—and... Georgina?"

"Yes. Evan was here; Georgina was around somewhere. On the golf course, I think."

"And Caspian, that's your youngest son?"

"Yes. He's my son with Vivien. The only child we have together."

I nodded and continued to make notes on my copy. Out of the corner of my eye, I could see that Kate and Tommy were doing the same.

"And Mr. and Mrs. Collins, Michael and Laura?"

"Yes, Michael is Vivien's son by her first marriage. Laura is his wife. They were both here, and so were the Margolises. Alicia is Vivien's daughter; Jeffery Margolis is her husband."

"These last two, Jackson the gardener and Moore the butler." I looked up at him. "Both here?"

He nodded.

"And Carriere, you're sure he wasn't here?"

"Yes, I'm sure."

I leaned back in the Chesterfield, sucked on the tip of my pencil, and stared down at the paper.

"I'm wondering, Mr. Martan," I said, without looking up from the list, "what all these people do for a living—not the staff members, of course; the others. Why are they here? I know it's a weekend, but other than the resort and the tourism industry, there's not a lot of work on the island. How do they make a living?"

I looked up just in time to see a discomfited look cross his face. It was there only for a second, but it told me more than I figured he wanted me to know. He was keeping them all.

"Leo, my son, is a stockbroker—" He coughed as he said it. It was almost as if the words choked him. "Excuse me. He's a stockbroker. Does most of his business from here, via the Internet. Cas—that's Caspian—is only nineteen. He's a freshman at Georgetown. He's home for fall break. Evan is in real estate…. No. He's not. He's a lazy, no good—he's not working right now. Michael is the general manager at the Windward Resort where you're staying; the family owns it. And Vivien's daughter's husband Jeffery is in banking, I think. None of the women work, at least not in the general sense of the word."

What the hell does he mean by that? I wondered. But I wasn't given the opportunity to find out. There was a knock at the door, and Moore opened it just far enough to look in.

"The lady from the police is here for Mr. Starke, sir."

I got to my feet. "Thank you, sir," I said to Martan. "That will do for now. I'll want to see everyone tomorrow morning, first together as a group, then individually. We'll also need to fingerprint everyone for purposes of elimination, should the need arise. If you could pass the word on to them, make sure everybody is here, including—" I looked at the list again "—Carriere, when we arrive, which should be around ten. That will give everyone time to get breakfast. Right now, I want to go and look at Gabrielle's room."

Daisy Patel was not at all what I was expecting. She was perhaps forty-five or forty-six years old, no more than five foot four, attractive, but slim as a rail and all business; she was also very good at her job, something that both surprised and delighted me.

She was waiting for us in the foyer. Tommy Quinn made the introductions.

"You're the tech I met earlier," I realized suddenly, "at the scene."

She nodded. We shook hands; her grip was firm, strong, and lasted no more than a second before she withdrew her hand and involuntarily wiped it on her pant leg. I smiled at her; she shrugged, not the slightest bit embarrassed by her own obvious distaste for human contact.

"How do you want to do this?" she asked.

"What did you find in the girl's room?"

"I tell you what. Here are my notes. Diagrams and photos of the scene and her rooms. Why don't you take a look at those first, and then we'll go up there and I'll walk you through it. That would be the best approach."

I looked through the photos and glanced through her notes, pleased to see her professional approach to her work. When I was done I handed the folder to Kate.

When she was done too, the four of us donned booties and latex gloves. I opened my iPad and took out my stylus, and Quinn removed the tape that blocked access to Gabrielle Martan's suite of rooms.

The door led into a small foyer that gave way to a spacious living room, a small kitchen, a huge bedroom, and a bathroom that was almost as big; all were located on the south side of house.

I turned on the lights and looked around. "Just give me a minute before we begin. I need to get a feel for the place," I said to Quinn and Patel. Kate already knew my methods and had, over the years, developed a set of her own that closely mirrored them.

The rooms were luxurious, and decorated from a palette of pastel colors: pink, blue, yellow, and white, lots of white.

The living-room furniture was all white; even the decorations where white: milk-glass decanters, vases, and bowls on the sideboards, several milk-glass bottles of various shapes and sizes and two fruit dishes on the coffee table, all obviously old, vintage at least. The walls were a pale shade of lemon; the drapes that hung by the French windows were striped in pastel shades of blue, pink, and lemon. The carpet was the palest shade of powder blue; there was a small section close to the center of the room that was missing. I could guess why.

We stood side by side in the foyer and took stock of the living room, then I led the others into the bedroom, which was almost identical in size, and where French windows ran almost the entire width of the room, as they did in the living room. The covers were missing from the bed, but I assumed that, like the furnishings, they were white, custom made, and expensive, just like the drapes drawn over the window.

"Is this how you found it? There's not a stick out of place. It doesn't even look lived in.

And I'm not seeing the usual mess of fingerprint powder."

"Pretty much," she replied. "The suite was cleaned this morning, around ten o'clock, ten thirty. We didn't talk to the housekeeper. She'd already left when we arrived. As far as fingerprint powder, I use a magnetic material. It's easy to clean up. All I need is a magnet. Can you imagine the mess the colored stuff would have made in here? You'd never be able to get the place clean again."

"Prints?" I asked.

"The usual. I'll need to print the family and staff to eliminate everyone I can."

I nodded. "And what time did you arrive?"

"We got the call at 2:45 and flew straight here. We got here just after 3:30. The doctor arrived at 4:05. You arrived at 4:55—the first time," she said dryly.

What the hell is her problem?

"The piece of carpet—blood?" I nodded toward the bare patch.

"Yes. A single spot. Tiny. If we hadn't been looking for it, we would have missed it."

I looked at Quinn. He was staring at the bare spot.

"What else?" I asked.

"There was a condom wrapper under the edge of the bed. It must have been put there

47

sometime after the room was cleaned... or not, if the housekeeper missed it, though I don't see how she could have. The bed was made up. I had it stripped and the covers bagged and tagged when I found the condom wrapper. Everything is in Charlotte Amalie, at the forensic center. We'll run DNA tests on the blood to make sure it's hers, but I doubt we'll get the results back anytime before Christmas. We'll run the bedding for hair and fibers, and we'll print the wrapper. You should have those results sometime tomorrow. I'll make sure you do."

I nodded. "How about the bathroom?"

"Nothing. Clean."

"The drains?"

She nodded. "Sinks, bath, and shower. Jerry removed the traps and covers and swabbed to a depth of eighteen inches; all clean—pristine, in fact. We tested the swabs. No blood. The same with the traps."

"The blood spot. What were your first impressions?"

"Not spatter. A drip, I think. It was resting on top of one of the wool fibers. It probably fell from the trickle by her ear when she was moved."

"Any idea where it might have happened?"

"Not specifically, but probably somewhere close to the center of the room; in one of the chairs, maybe."

48

"I agree," I said. "If she'd been standing, there would have been more blood spatter. Sitting, most if not all of it would have landed on her clothing. Still…." I looked around at where the section of carpet had been cut away. "Was there any sign the carpet had been cleaned in any way?"

"Washed, you mean? No. It was dry and, as you can see, clean. The single spot was all there was."

"Luminol? Black light?"

She looked sharply at me. "Of course," she snapped.

"Of course you did. Sorry. How about her clothing? Have you had a chance to inspect that yet?"

"Not yet. It went with the body to Charlotte Amalie. I'll get to it as soon as I get back there. You'll have the results of that too."

I ignored her tone. "Who found the body, and how?"

"I'm told she was found by the gardener. I don't know his name, nor do I particularly care. I just do my job and leave the clever stuff to the detectives." She turned and looked at me. "And to you, I guess."

What the hell is wrong with you, lady?

"Okay, Ms. Patel. Out with it. Who kicked your cat, and why do you have your knife into me?"

49

She sighed, shook her head. "It's not you, Mr. Starke. I wasn't asked to do this. I was ordered, dragged away from... from... my daughter's giving birth as we speak. She shouldn't be. She's at risk. I should be there, but I'm stuck here until God only knows when—but that's no concern of yours. Let's get on with it. The sooner we're through, the sooner I can get back."

Damn. That's on me. "Have you called? How's she doing?"

"So far so good. She's in labor, but...."

"Okay. Do you have anyone here that can fill in for you? I need about an hour with you tonight, and I need to get everyone fingerprinted in the morning. Do you have anyone here who can do that?"

"No. Just me. When we finished with the scene and her rooms I sent everyone else home."

"Damn. It needs to be done by a sworn officer."

"I can do it," Quinn said. "If you'll leave the scanner here I'll transmit the files and see that the machine gets back to you as soon as I can."

She brightened visibly.

I nodded. "Let's get on with it then, but before we do, do you have a way to get back to St. Thomas?"

"I'll make a call. I have a friend with a boat who can come and get me."

50

"A boat? Won't that take all night?"

"It's a fast boat, and the sea is calm right now. It'll only be ninety minutes or so."

"That will put you in St. Thomas around one thirty. I think we can do better than that. I noticed there's a helicopter at the back of the house. I assume it's Leo's. I'm sure he wouldn't mind giving you a ride. Tommy, would you mind asking him to join us, please?"

They were back just a couple of minutes later, but the helicopter—it belonged to Leo Jr.—was a no-go. The pilot was in St. Croix until morning and the only other person with a license was Leo Jr. himself, and he was nowhere to be found. Daisy Patel would have to take the boat.

Leo Sr. left. Said he'd be in his office if we needed him.

"I'm sorry Ms. Patel," I said after he'd gone. "We tried. Make the call to your friend." And she did.

I walked to the French windows, opened the door, and walked out onto the balcony, being very careful about where I put my feet. The balcony was wide—huge, in fact, probably ten feet from the doors to the rail, and it stretched the entire width of the two rooms. I took a small tape measure from my pocket. The rail was solid stone, or maybe concrete, and slightly less than forty inches high. Just below the belt for me, but for a girl some six to eight inches shorter....

I leaned over the rail and looked down at the tent below. It looked tiny. *Damn. That's a hell of a drop.*

I walked the length of the balcony, inching my way along, looking for anything that might provide a clue as to what might have happened: nothing.

I looked across the gap that separated Gabrielle's balcony from the identical one next door. They were about eight to ten feet apart. It would be quite a jump, but not because of the distance: the rails were narrow, hardly jumping-off or landing spots, but… not impossible. *Hell, you never know.*

Once more I looked down at the small white tent below and wondered: *Was she conscious? Did she know what was happening to her?* I sure as hell hoped not.

I heaved a sigh and looked up, out over the golf course. The lights of the resort were visible just beyond the moonlit fairway, and a few degrees to the west I could see those of the wharf and marina and the boats, and beyond that the ocean, silver and sparkling in the moonlight: the view was breathtaking. I turned away, shaking my head, wistful, wishing….

"Ms. Patel," I said, reentering the living room, blinking a little in the sudden light. "Did Dr. Matheson make any mention of a time of death?"

"No, but it would have had to have been sometime after noon; I believe she had lunch with her father."

"And you say you got the call at 2:45. Tommy, how about you?"

"The same. We rode over together. I took a quick look at the scene and turned it over to Ms. Patel."

"So the gardener discovered the body; do you know when? Do you know his name?" Kate asked, leaning over the balcony.

"His name's Jackson. I'm not sure exactly when he found her. I didn't talk to him."

"What? Why the hell not?"

He looked at her as if she'd slapped him in the face.

"Whoa, lady. I didn't talk to him because no sooner had I looked at the body than I was sent on a wild goose chase after Sherlock Holmes here. If you—"

"Okay," I interrupted him. "Okay. That's enough. I don't need you two squabbling, so don't even start—"

"Did you talk to anybody, anybody at all?" Kate demanded.

"Only Mr. Martan."

"You were here for no more than thirty minutes," Kate said. "You talked to no one but

Martan, and yet you decided it was suicide. How come?"

Yeah. How come. That's something that's been bothering me.

He looked away. "I just didn't see how it could have been anything else! There were no marks on her that I could see, just the gash on her forehead, which I assumed had been caused by the fall. No defensive wounds, nothing under her nails... and there was no one else here other than a few family members: father, mother, brothers. What else could it have been? The place is a fortress. You know that."

"The indicators were there," Kate said. "You just didn't—"

"Okay. That's enough." I could see the color rising in Quinn's face, so I cut her off before things could get any more out of hand.

"You said that no sooner had you looked at the body.... What time was that?" I asked him. "How long after you landed?"

"I dunno. Thirty minutes. Maybe a little more. I barely had time to inspect the scene before they were out here, Mr. Martan and that butler of his. Which is another reason I didn't see—"

"So four o'clock, then?"

"About that time, yeah."

Hmmm. I'm not getting this. I need to know what time the gardener found her.

54

It was too far and too time-consuming to go looking for Martan, so I took out my iPhone and dialed his number. He answered on the second ring.

"Hi, sorry to bother you sir, but I need to talk to the gardener. Could you have Moore send him up here, please?"

"He's not on the property, I'm afraid."

"Ah. Well when will he be here?"

"Tomorrow morning, presumably, when his next shift starts."

"Fine. Would you please make sure he's available when I get here, then? I want to talk to him as soon as I can."

He said that he would; I said goodbye, and then turned to Kate.

"Well, you heard that. I'm not understanding the timeline here. Tommy arrives at three thirty and by four he's at the resort with Leo Martan."

"Yeah," she said, "and there's more, I think. She was still dressed for bed. We know the room was cleaned by ten thirty, eleven at the latest, and she could well have been in her pajamas while that was being done, but…." She looked up from the photos, waved one of them at Patel. You said she had lunch with her father. If so, she wouldn't have been dressed like this. Her fiancé wasn't here, so she must have been having an affair, which would account for the condom

55

wrapper and how she was dressed. So at noon, if she was with her father—why didn't he mention it?"

"Let's find out," I said, fishing for my phone again. After I hung up, I looked around at the others. "She didn't have lunch with him. She was supposed to, but she called and said she had a headache, and took a rain check."

I looked at Kate, then Quinn, then Patel, and then I watched a slow smile grow on Kate's face.

"Our Gabby was a naughty girl," she said. "Either that, or her boyfriend snuck in, gave her one, then whacked her over the head, tossed her over the rail, and then snuck out again. Hardly seems likely, does it. Which begs the question: Who was she screwing? And why the condom? In these enlightened times, fiancés don't generally use them. They rely on other methods. So neither of them would have them around, and if she was on the pill or something she probably wouldn't have required her visitor to use one either, which means he came prepared in that he didn't want to leave his DNA, and that smacks of premeditation, right?"

There was no denying her logic. We didn't know if she was having an affair, but I sure as hell would find out. But even then what we'd have would only be circumstantial; it could still have been the fiancé.

56

"We need to find out if she was on some sort of birth control," I said.

"Maybe not," Kate said suddenly, and then she turned and walked into the bathroom, returning a moment later waving a pack of contraceptive patches. "She was on the patch."

"Okay, so that provides us with more questions, not the least of which is: When did she take that swan dive?" I said it to nobody in particular. "I find it hard to believe she was lying out there in the heat of the day and no one spotted her. Dressed as she was, she'd attract attention, and quickly. Yes?"

I looked around the group. Kate shrugged. Quinn shook his head, frowning. Patel had her eyes closed as if deep in thought. "Ms. Patel?"

She opened her eyes, blinked twice, then shook her head and said, "Body temperature isn't going to help. She was very warm. No rigor. Either she wasn't dead more than a few minutes, or the heat of the day and rocks she was lying on interfered with the natural cooling process. There's a window of opportunity between eleven in the morning and when the gardener found her. That could be as long as three hours."

"True. We'll get a better idea when we talk to him, and the ME, in the morning. Well," I said, taking a last look around, "there's not a whole lot more we can do until tomorrow. Let's get out of here, shall we?"

"Here's my cell number," Patel said, handing me her card. "All being well with Miranda—that's my daughter—I'll be in the office by eight thirty. Call me anytime. I'll drop everything," she added dryly.

I couldn't help but smile at her, and she softened.

"I'm sorry. That was uncalled for. You've been very kind. Were it not for you, I'd still be here in the morning. In the meantime, if you'll have someone take me back to the Windward, I'll leave you my fingerprint scanner."

"Tommy?" I asked, looking over at him.

He nodded. "Sure. Whenever you're ready," he told her.

"Where are you meeting your boat?" I asked her.

"At the Dive Shop at the wharf near the resort." She looked at her watch. "He should be there soon, I think."

"Tommy," I said. "How about you drop Kate and me off at the resort first, and then take Ms. Patel to get her things and the scanner, and then drop her off at the wharf."

"That will work."

"Okay, let me have a quick word with Martan, and then we'll go."

I found Martan still in his office. He looked tired, which was no surprise.

"I have just a couple of questions, sir, if you don't mind."

"Of course not. Fire away."

"It's about the folks who weren't present today. Are you absolutely sure they weren't on the property when Gabrielle was killed? I'm thinking in particular about her fiancé."

"Gabrielle told me he had a charter and wouldn't be back until late tonight. I can't confirm that, but I didn't see him at all."

"Charter?"

"Yes. He owns a boat. That's how he makes his living."

"And he keeps it... where?"

"At the wharf, of course. Close to the resort. That's where he gets most of his clients."

I nodded, scribbled a quick note into the iPad, and then continued. "Gabrielle was supposed to have lunch with you, but she didn't. Do you know if she ate breakfast?"

"Yes, she did. It was taken to her rooms."

"And at what time was that, and what did it consist of?"

"It was at eight thirty, as always. Scrambled eggs, orange juice, and coffee."

"I don't suppose you know if she ate it all?"

"As a matter of fact, I do. I happened to be in the kitchen when the maid brought her tray down. She ate the eggs and drank the coffee. The juice, no."

I nodded, made more notes. "The suite of rooms next to Gabrielle's, who occupies it?"

"Alicia and Jeffery. That is, my wife's daughter and her husband."

Hmmm. I wonder where they were when Gabby took to the skies.

"Well then." I closed my iPad. "I think I have what I need for now. If you would, please make sure everyone is here in the morning. Will the people who were absent today be here?"

"They should be. Tomorrow is Sunday."

I left him sitting behind his desk and went to join the others, who were already in the car waiting. I relayed the breakfast information to Daisy Patel and asked her to make sure the ME got it before he began the autopsy. Five minutes later, Quinn dropped Kate and me off at the resort.

It was after eleven that evening when I joined Amanda and my father by the pool. Kate didn't join us. Said something about sleep. Me? I was too wired for bed. I poured myself a huge glass of Laphroaig over an ice cube and flopped down on a lounger beside my wife. *Ha. My wife.* I took a long drink of the scotch and savored the fire as it sank down through me.

Amanda reached out, took my hand, squeezed it, and said, "So how was it?"

"I'm... not sure. I haven't talked to anyone yet. Well, Leo, but that's all. The only thing I know for sure is that somebody inside that house, probably in that family, hit the girl over the head and threw her off the balcony."

Amanda got up and seated herself on the edge of my lounger, then leaned in and kissed me gently. She tasted of sweet white wine, and I was suddenly overcome by a feeling like none I'd ever experienced before, something akin to fear, but the exact opposite. It was like the bottom had dropped out of my stomach. Weird, but nice, and I liked it.

My father rose from his chair. "I'll leave you two newlyweds alone then."

"You don't need to go," I began, but Amanda gave me a sly dig with her elbow. August caught it, and smiled.

"Yes, I think maybe I do. I'll see you kids in the morning. Have a good night."

We stayed there by the pool for maybe another hour, talking, whispering together, about what I really don't remember. What I do remember is that I had never been, and probably never will be again, happier than I was that night. My life was complete, and Gabrielle Martan was absolutely not a part of it.

Chapter 5

Sunday November 13. Early Morning

"Good morning Mrs. Starke," I said, placing a cup of coffee on the nightstand beside her.

She blinked once, then opened her eyes wide and sat bolt upright in bed. "Oh my God. That's me," she said, as the covers fell away to reveal... nope, I'm not going there.

She laughed and grabbed the coffee with both hands, staring at me over the rim of the cup as I sat down beside her.

"What time is it?" she asked, squinting in the early morning light.

"Just after seven. Do you want breakfast? I can order it in."

"Ooh yes please. Pancakes, I want pancakes, and syrup. Lots of syrup, and an omelet." I smiled, shook my head in amazement. She never was one to count calories, and she never suffered for it either.

I still remember a time when, lovely as she is, I couldn't stand the sight of her. She is... no, she *was* an anchor at Channel 7 TV, and she did a number on me, on air. I swore I'd never forgive her for it, but here we are. Funny how times and situations change.

"Hey," she said, breaking into my thoughts. "You still with me, or what?"

I took the cup from her and kissed the tip of her nose. "You betcha. So, pancakes, syrup, and an omelet, right?"

She nodded, slipped her hands around my neck, and pulled. "Yes, but first...."

She never did get her pancakes, or the omelet. By the time she was done with me it was almost eight o'clock and I had to get moving. I left her lying in bed and headed for the shower. She was still there when I came out.

"I'll see you later," I said as I kissed her goodbye. "Take care of Dad and Rose. I'll try to get back in time for dinner, okay?"

She sighed, nodded, and then rolled over onto her belly: damn, I almost didn't make it out the door.

Kate and Quinn were already waiting for me when I walked out into the sunshine. They were sitting together with Bob, Jacque, and Tim in the clubhouse, drinking coffee.

"You coming with us, Bob?" I asked.

"Sure, if I can help. Kate's already filled me in. Hell, we were up half the night talking about it. What do you need me to do?"

"I'm not sure yet. If Martan was able to get everyone together, Kate and I will conduct the interviews. I'll need you to work with Tommy Quinn. Fingerprints and the like."

He nodded. "What are you thinking, Harry?"

"If you're asking if I have any ideas about who might have killed her, other than that it has to be someone in that house, I don't." I looked around, caught the eye of one of the servers, and waved her over.

"I need coffee please, fresh and strong." I waited while she fetched it, asked her to leave the pot, and then continued.

"Tim. I've got a list of people I need you to run checks on. What do you think?" I asked, handing him the four sheets of paper. He flipped through them, nodding, humming to himself, constantly adjusting his glasses with his finger.

"Easy enough. Will an hour be okay?"

I looked at him, surprised. I shouldn't have been, but I always was. "That's fine. I'll need four hard copies, if you can."

"Hard copies," he snorted. "I'll send them to everyone's iPads. How much time do you have?"

"We need to be at the house by ten, earlier if possible. And yes, the iPad is good, but I'll also need at least one hard copy. Can you do that?"

He looked at his watch. "Of course. I'll have 'em to you by nine." And then he got up from the table and left, wandering away, never once taking his eyes from the paper. I marveled at how he managed to avoid every obstacle in his way, even the pool, seemingly without looking.

"Okay," I said, dragging myself back into the moment. "Here's what needs to be done. Take notes. There's a list of about a dozen people that need to be fingerprinted and interviewed. As I said, Bob, you and Tommy will do the printing. Kate and I will conduct the interviews. I also need to talk to the ME." I looked at my watch: almost eight thirty. "He should have started the post by now. I'll give him another hour and then call him. I'll do that on speakerphone so you all will be in the loop. In the meantime, let's get comfortable and go over what we have."

I looked at the coffee pot. It was already empty. I waved a hand and attracted the attention of our server again.

"Would you get us a refill, please? And I need something to eat. Anyone else?" No one did, so I ordered some banana fritters and French toast for myself. "Oh, and one more thing. Can you take some pancakes and a plain omelet to Mrs. Starke in the cottage?" Kate and Bob tried to hide their smiles, and I suddenly felt extremely self-conscious. *Okay, so calling her that is going to take some getting used to.*

The food came and I gobbled it down like a dog. When I was done, I pushed away my plate, poured myself some more coffee, and opened my iPad.

"Okay, Jacque," I said. "If you would take notes, we have about thirty minutes before I should call the ME. So let's begin with a list of suspects, and, Jacque, if you would send them to everyone's device when we're done, that would help a lot."

"No problem." She flipped open the cover on her iPad and sat looking at me expectantly, stylus in hand.

I flipped through the pages Martan had given to me, and then through the screens on my iPad until I found the file with the notes I'd made at the scene.

"Alright."

1. *Gabrielle Martan was murdered sometime after eleven yesterday morning and before three in the afternoon.*

2. *The body was found by Albert Jackson, the gardener at the mansion. At what time, we don't yet know.*

3. *The killer has to be either someone in the family, or close to it, or on the staff. They include:*

   - *Her father, Leopold Martan*

   - *Her stepmother, Vivien Martan*

   - *Her brother, Leo Jr., and his wife, Lucy*

   - *Her brother, Evander "Evan," not married, but has a girlfriend, Georgina*

- *Her brother Caspian, single*
- *Her stepbrother, Michael Collins, and his wife Laura*
- *Her stepsister, Alicia Margolis, and her husband Jeffery*
- *Last but not least, her fiancé, Sebastian Carriere, charter boat owner and captain*
- *There's also the butler, Victor Moore, and the gardener, Jackson*

I read it all aloud, then looked up. "I make that a solid dozen suspects, fourteen including the butler—"

"Hah," Kate interrupted. "This is an easy one: the butler did it."

"But you don't mean you suspect Martan and his wife?" Quinn asked, obviously taken aback.

"Come on, Tommy. You know better than to ask questions like that," I said. "Everyone's a suspect until we can eliminate them."

"But Martan insisted you be brought in. If he hadn't, we would have said the death was a suicide."

"Look, I don't think it was him, or his wife, but they stay on the list until we're sure."

"Well, okay then." He shook his head, obviously unhappy about it.

"Tommy," I said after a pause, "give. What are you thinking?"

"I'm thinking we can't afford to upset the man." He saw the look I was giving him. "I know, I know, but he carries more weight in these islands than a freight train does in Philly."

"Yeah, well. I don't give a rat's ass about who he is. It was his choice to involve me, so he can live with it. Now, on to better things.

"Someone, it would seem, was having an affair with the victim. CSI found a condom wrapper under the bed. Could have been the fiancé's, but why? She was using the patch... well, we found a package of them in the bathroom. We won't know for sure until I talk to the ME, but if so, why the condom? If she was having an affair, who was the lucky guy? We need to find out.

"We need to establish a timeline, as near as we can, from when she ate breakfast at eight thirty until the time of her death.... Hey, Tim. What do you need?"

He was back.

"Not a thing," he said, "but if you'll check your e-mail you'll find a file with the information you asked for. It's pretty big, but it's all there—well, almost all of it. There were a couple of things I have to wait for, but—"

"Okay, okay, Tim. I get it. Great work, and quick."

"Not really. I had the socials and birthdates, so that made running the searches very easy. It was just a matter of downloading it all, sorting it, and… what? Seriously, what?"

I was laughing at him. Once he got started there was no stopping him.

"Nothing, Tim. Thanks, but now go find Sammie and enjoy the day. Keep your phone handy, though. I may need you. Oh, but before you go—was there anything or anyone who stuck out?"

"Was there ever. Leo Jr. is under investigation by the FBI for investment fraud. Both brothers are broke. So is the boyfriend, Carrier—he couldn't borrow a quarter for a phone call. The butler is an anomaly. He's clean, but has no credit history, which is strange, seeing as he spent seven years in the Navy, as a *Seal*, no less. It's all there."

"Thanks, Tim. And by the way, it's Carri*ere*, not Carrier. Now go enjoy yourself. I'll call you if I need you."

He grinned, nodded, and left, whistling.

"Okay. It's about time I called the ME. You guys ready?" They were, and I dialed Wilson's number. Surprise, surprise, he answered himself.

I told him he would be on speaker, and after I made the introductions, I suggested he start the ball rolling.

"I know you're in a hurry for some sort of result," he began. My heart took a nosedive, but it was okay. He was just doing a little CYA.

"I haven't yet completed my examination, but I probably have everything you need, at least in the short term."

I heaved a silent sigh of relief.

"The girl died as a result of massive trauma to the back of the skull—from the fall. The blunt-force trauma to her forehead was caused just prior to her death, not by the fall: there are no particulates in or around the wound—no stone or rock dust. That blow probably rendered her unconscious, but was not in itself life-threatening. I believe she was probably sitting when she received it. Whoever did it was standing over her. There is low-impact blood spatter, several spots, on the hem of her housecoat, or whatever that flimsy thing she was wearing is called, in her lap, as it were. I'd say most of it, in fact."

"PMI?" I asked.

"Due to the heat of the rocks, on which she must have lain for at least an hour, and the heat of the sun, it was difficult to determine. When she arrived here last night it was almost six o'clock. Lividity was fully developed, but not set. As you probably know, digestion stops when the body dies, but the contents of her stomach had already moved into the upper small intestine, which indicates a time of death roughly three to four hours after her last meal. Do you know what time that was, Mr. Starke?"

"Uh-huh. She had scrambled eggs and coffee at eight thirty yesterday morning."

70

"Hmmm, so, knowing that, and taking into account the state of lividity, I'll hazard a guess that she died some four to six hours after eating breakfast, say between noon and two. Sorry I can't be more specific."

"That's fine, Doctor. It gives us a place to start. Now, what about sexual activity?"

"There was no semen, if that's what you're asking, but sexual intercourse did take place sometime in the twelve hours prior to her death."

"I know you haven't had time for a blood analysis," I said, "but I believe she was on some sort of birth control. Did you find…?"

"Yes. There was an Ortho Evra contraceptive patch on her right buttock. You wouldn't have seen it, not without moving the body. It would have been hidden by her underwear."

"So there would have been no need for a condom?"

"Well, yes and no. It would depend how well she knew her sexual partner. If she knew him well, no; if it was a one-night stand, she probably would have insisted on one being used to protect herself from STDs.

"I found nothing under her fingernails, and there were no signs of defensive wounds. The blow to her forehead must have taken her by surprise. I still have to finish up, but I doubt there'll be anything more; not soon, anyway. Tox screens will take at least a week. DNA, maybe a month. If I find anything else I think is untoward,

I'll call you. So, unless you have any more questions, Mr. Starke. I need to wrap this up. I have two more waiting, both diving accidents."

"No, Doctor, I think I'm good for now. If I do think of anything else I'll get back to you, though. Thank you for doing this so quickly."

I disconnected the call and sat back in my chair, put my feet up on the table, and put my head back.

"That condom wrapper bothers me," I told the ceiling fan. "She wouldn't have allowed her fiancé to use one, right? Like washing your feet with your socks on." I looked at Kate. She shook her head.

"And Daisy Patel didn't find the condom itself, so it was either flushed, or the partner took it with him, which is what I would have done if…. Well I *wouldn't*—kill anyone, I mean—not like that. So if it was someone she knew, and it had to be, why the condom? Hell, maybe he didn't know she was on the patch. But… if she knew him well enough to have intercourse with him, she'd tell him, right?" Again I looked at Kate, then at Jacque.

"Not necessarily," Jacque said. "Things are not as they used to be. She could have been screwin' d'butler."

"Yeah, right. Now that's real funny," I said, but then…. I thought about the Christopher Walken lookalike and said, "Hell, I dunno. It takes all sorts, I guess."

I looked at my watch. It was 9:45.

"We'd better get on up there, I suppose," I said, and sucked down the last of my cold coffee and ate the last of my French toast, also cold.

"Jacque. If you could get those notes to us as soon as you can…."

She nodded. "Give me fifteen minutes to sort and edit it."

I took a minute to go to the cottage and tell Amanda goodbye, and we all climbed into Quinn's borrowed SUV—apparently there were no cruisers on Calypso Key.

Chapter 6

It was a few minutes after ten when we parked outside the front entrance to the Martan home. The butler, Moore, met us at the front door and ushered us into what he described as the drawing room.

Drawing room? Do people do that anymore? Draw, I mean. Yeah, yeah, I know. It's the with*drawing room. I'm being facetious. Come on, Harry; stop screwing around. Get your mind back on track. Think suspects.*

Not so easy. I looked at Moore, and the more I did, the more inclined I was to agree with Kate; maybe the butler did do it. Joking, joking. Sort of.

Anyway, the *drawing* room was packed. It was a big room, but even so, having more than a dozen people in it made it seem very crowded.

"Ah, you're here," Leo Martan said, making his way across the room toward us, his hand extended for me to shake.

"Everyone is here, with the exception of Carriere. Something about his boat, I believe. I—"

"One moment, if you don't mind, Mr. Martan," I interrupted. "Who else is missing?"

"No one."

"How about the gardener?"

74

"He's here. He's over there." He pointed to a tall, muscular man standing alone by the window.

"I need for Mr. Carriere to be present," I said. "Where can we find him?"

"He'll be on his boat, I should think, but—"

"Please, sir. I said I needed everyone. Tommy, Bob," I said, turning to them. "Go get him. Don't take no for an answer. Arrest him, if you have to." They left, and I turned again to Leo Martan. If he was expecting an explanation, he wasn't going to get one. I looked around the room at the sea of faces; there was not a smile among them. That, I supposed, could have been because of the loss of Gabrielle, or maybe because of my aggressive action. If the latter, well, I'd made my point and established control.

Most of them were sitting; three, including Jackson, the gardener, were standing at the far end of the room. Kate and I were just inside the door. Martan was on Kate's right, Moore on my left.

Martan lost no more time. He made the introductions and then took a seat next to his wife; Kate and I remained standing.

"Well, good morning everyone," I began. "I want to say a few words before Lieutenant Gazzara and I begin the preliminary interviews—"

"I'm sorry." It was Leo Jr. who interrupted me. "I want to know what the hell this is all about. You," he said to me, "aren't even a police officer, and the lieutenant has no standing in the Virgin Islands. I have no time for this. I have things to do. I'm leaving."

Martan rose to his feet. His face was white, rigid with anger.

"These people are here at my request, Leo," he said, "and their investigation is fully sanctioned by Commissioner Walker. You will treat them with the respect they deserve, which they've earned. Now sit down and shut your damn mouth." The man was shaking with rage. His eldest son did as he was told and sat down.

"Please continue, Mr. Starke." Martan sat down again. The room was deathly quiet.

"To continue," I said. "Gabrielle Martan was murdered—"

"Bullshit," Leo Jr. said loudly. "All right, all right." This as his father again began to rise from his seat.

"Gabrielle," I said, watching each of them carefully, "was murdered by someone here, in this room, and I'm including Sebastian Carriere in that statement. One of you killed her." I paused, looking around the room, looking for the slightest sign of a reaction that might tell me something. Two of the women, Vivien Martan and Alicia Margolis, squirmed uncomfortably, but that was all. Leo Jr.'s eyes were narrowed and there was a half smile on his lips. *Arrogant, smart-ass son of a bitch.*

I knew why. During the ride up to the house I'd opened Tim's file and scanned through the contents, and oh how interesting they were.

"We've allowed thirty minutes each for the preliminary interviews," I continued. "It may take longer than that, or not so much. That being said, I don't want to keep you all hanging around here. Lieutenant Gazzara has made a list of the order in which we'll take you, so that will give you a rough idea of the time. In the meantime, you can go, but please keep your phones handy; we'll call you when we're ready for you. Before we begin, however, I need a quick word with Mr. Jackson, and then we'll start the interviews, and we might as well begin with you, *Junior*, since it seems you have better things to do."

No, I made no attempt to hide my dislike for the man, or my sarcastic tone of voice. He glared back at me. The smile was gone. His face was a mask—of anger? Hate? Probably both, but who the hell cared? Gabrielle certainly didn't.

They each took a copy of Kate's list and left; only the two Leos and Jackson remained.

Martan had put his office at our disposal, and it was there we conducted the interviews, the gardener first.

Albert Jackson was not quite what you'd expect of a seasoned gardener but then, as he told me, he was more of a groundskeeper than a man of the soil. His job was, in fact, to keep the grounds around the Mount in pristine condition, and he had several employees to help him do that: mowing, weeding, etcetera.

He was forty-two years old and single, and he was dressed as if for the golf course next door; tan pants and a pale blue shirt. The only evidence of his life outdoors was his tan. His face and arms were the color of tobacco; his blond hair had turned almost white due to long days spent under the sun. He was not a handsome man. The huge, bushy eyebrows, piercing black eyes, and thin, mean-looking lips reminded me of a wharf rat.

"Good morning, Mr. Jackson," I began, indicating for him to sit. "We will be recording the interview." I picked up the digital recorder, turned it on, and set it back on the desk in front of him.

I stated the usual details for the recorder—time, place, those present, etc., and then I began.

"I understand you found Gabrielle yesterday, and I know it must have been a terrible experience, and I feel for you. However, I need a little information."

"Of course. Anything I can do to help."

"The first thing I need to know is exactly what time it was when you found her. I see you're not wearing a watch, but did you by any chance make a note of the time?"

"Yes, of course. I use my iPhone. When I called Mr. Martan it was 2:09."

I tapped the time into my iPad, looked up at him, and said, "You say you called Mr. Martan. What exactly did you say to him?"

"I told him I'd found Gabrielle, and that she was dead, and I told him where. He came straight out of the front entrance."

"How long was it between when you called him and when he arrived at the scene?"

"Two, three minutes. No more than that."

"So that would have made the time 2:15, or thereabouts?"

He nodded. "I guess."

"No, Mr. Jackson. Don't guess. This is important."

"Well, I didn't check, but yeah, about 2:15. He was quick."

I shook my head, looked at Kate. She rolled her eyes. *Good job Jackson didn't see that.*

"Mr. Jackson," she said quietly. "Please, take us through the sequence of events, from when you found the body until... well, we'll see."

"Well, as I said, I was making my midday rounds... eh, I was a little late, but anyway. I rounded the end of the house and I saw her lying on the rocks. I ran to her, but I could see she was

dead. Her head was a mess, there was blood…
and… well, you know."

"You were late? Why was that?"

"One of the mowers broke down. I helped
Henry fix it."

"When you found her, did you touch
anything?" Kate asked.

"No. Well, I felt her neck to see if there
was a pulse, but there wasn't."

"You just said you knew she was dead, so
why did you do that?"

"I dunno. Saw it on TV, I guess. It just
seemed like the thing to do, you know?"

Kate nodded. "Go on, Mr. Jackson."

"Well, I got up off my knees, backed up a
few steps, and made the call to Mr. Martan."

"And you noted the time?"

He nodded.

"And Mr. Martan came immediately. Was
he alone?"

"No ma'am. Mrs. Vivien was with him."

"And their reactions?"

"Well, they were upset, of course. Mrs.
Vivien was having a fit; screaming, you know.
Well not exactly screaming, but making a lot of
noise. Mr. Martan… he was quiet, very quiet. He
hardly said anything at all. He kneeled down
beside her, and just looked at her, and… well,
then he—he got up, told me not to let anyone near

her, and then he went into the house. To call the police, I guess. He didn't say. They arrived maybe an hour or so later."

"So it was just after 2:15 when he made the call?" I asked.

"That's right."

"All right, Mr. Jackson," I said. "That will be all for now. We may want to talk to you later. You'll be here, yes?"

He nodded. "I'll be in the barn if you need me. I have an apartment above it."

I waited until he left and then said to Kate, "Okay. He seemed pretty sure about the time. If he's right, there was at least a thirty-minute delay before Martan called it in. That's not natural. A normal person's first reaction on finding the body of one of their children would be to call 911, immediately. Why didn't he? Also, I noticed earlier that he carries his cell phone on his belt. Why would he need to go into the house to make the call?"

"He was checking on someone," Kate said.

"Yeah, but who the hell was it... and why?"

"I think we should talk to him next. We need to find out before we talk to anyone else, don't you think?"

"Yeah. Let's get him in here. Junior can wait."

I made the call and asked Martan to join us.

Chapter 7

We were in Martan's office, so it felt a little weird when I asked him to sit, especially as Kate and I were seated behind his desk.

"I'll get right to it, Mr. Martan," I said. "We have a problem. Why did it take you so long to call emergency services after you saw the body?"

His mouth opened as if in protest, then he snapped it shut. I heard his teeth click together.

"I… I…. It didn't," he blustered. "I called it in as soon as I could, as soon as…." He trailed off, looked down at his hands, then back up at me defiantly.

I took my time, made him wait, stared down at my iPad. I wanted to make him as uncomfortable as possible. Out of the corner of my eye, I could see that Kate was playing along. She had him fixed with an unblinking stare. I slowly counted to twenty, to myself, and then I looked up at him, shaking my head slowly.

"No you didn't," I said quietly.

"I most certainly did."

"No you didn't," I repeated. "Jackson found the body at 2:09 exactly. He noted the time on his iPhone when he called you. Your call was recorded in Charlotte Amalie at exactly 2:42. That's a thirty-three-minute gap. Jackson also

83

said you were with him for less than five minutes. What were you doing during the twenty-eight minutes between when you left Jackson guarding the body and when you made the call. Mr. Martan?"

"I told you. I made the call as soon as I got back into the house. Jackson must have made a mistake."

"No. He didn't make a mistake. He was very specific. Now look, Mr. Martan. I'm here at your request. I expect you of all people to tell me the truth. If not, I'm not going to fool with you; I'm out of here. Understand?"

He nodded, dropped his chin, and stared down at his hands.

"Look," I said gently. "I know what you're trying to do. It won't work. Who are you trying to protect? Where did you go when you left Jackson?"

"I went… looking for Leo. My son."

I waited, but he didn't continue. He just continued to stare down at his hands.

"And?"

"They, Leo and Gabrielle, had had a huge fight just after breakfast. It was a carryover from the night before. They'd been at each other's throats for more than a month, and I thought maybe…."

"Go on."

"I thought... I thought he was here somewhere. The helicopter was still on the pad. He has a pilot, but the man was off. When that's the case, Leo flies it himself, so I thought he had to have been here, but he wasn't. There's no other way off the island, other than the boat, but that was still at the dock, so I assumed he'd gone out. I called him, but he didn't answer, not until much later that afternoon. He said he'd needed to get away for a while, that he'd taken the Sunfish and gone sailing.... That was when I told him about Gabby."

He looked up at me. I watched his eyes. He couldn't look me in the eye for more than a few seconds. Kate caught it too.

"And you believed him?" she asked.

He seemed startled by the question, but after a moment he said, "Why, yes. Why wouldn't I?"

"I get the distinct impression that you're worried about him," she said. "He's having money problems, isn't he?"

Again, the startled look. "No. Well... yes, he's...."

"He's under investigation for a whole litany of fraudulent stock deals, is what he is," I said, watching his eyes. *Not exactly true, but near enough.*

"Well, he has some financial problems, but nothing really serious; at least I don't think so. He *never* discusses his business with me."

"Why not?" Kate asked.

He shrugged, looked down at his hands again, and said, more to himself than to us, "One of those father-son things, I think. Claims he's always walking in my shadow; which he is, I suppose. Anyway. His dealings are his own. If he needs help from me, all he has to do is ask. But he never does, *never.*" That last part was said with some angst.

"So what were they arguing about?" I asked.

Again he shrugged and didn't look up. I figured he was trying not to give away his feelings, his thoughts. It wasn't working. The fact that he couldn't look me in the eye was a dead giveaway.

"The usual," he said. "Money. It's always about money."

We waited, but he said no more.

"Please, Mr. Martan," I said. "You're not making things any easier, for yourself, your son, or for us. You need to be candid with us. Please don't make us drag every little piece of information out of you."

He looked up at me, his face set, and he straightened up in his seat and took on a whole new attitude. He became the Leo Martan who would take no garbage from anyone.

"My son, Leo," he said—and now he looked me right in the eye—"and my other son, Evander, are both disappointments to me, Mr. Starke. They are both weak willed, lazy, easily led, and have never made a good decision in their lives, either of them. Evan is dead broke and out of work, living here on handouts, and Leo's business is a disaster—I know; I keep an eye on it—his private life is no better, and his wife... she's a gold digger, man hungry, and... well, you'll see for yourself when you meet her. But let me say this: for all my son's faults, he loved his sister. They bickered back and forth, and I know he wanted her to give him money, but he would never have harmed her. They have always slapped each other around—she more than him—but that was it."

"Could it have been an accident during the argument?" Kate asked. "Could he have lost control and hit her harder than he intended?"

"Anything is possible, I suppose.... I don't know. I've been worrying about it all night long. I hope not. I really do hope not."

"So do I," I said, "because a single unintended blow to the head is one thing; tipping her over the balcony after turns it into murder. Okay, enough about your son for now. Let's move along. Let's talk about Gabrielle."

87

"Of course. What would you like to know?"

"First, who benefits from her death? How much money is involved?"

"Money? I'm not sure I understand."

"Well, from what I understand, she was quite wealthy, correct?"

"Not right now. Not until her twenty-fifth birthday next month. She has an allowance, from her trust. Her mother set it up before she died. She did it for all three of our children. It's enough for her to live very well, but not enough to be worth killing her for."

"And on her birthday?" Kate asked.

He looked sideways at her, his eyes narrowed. "She would have become extremely wealthy."

I sighed. He took notice. "She would have attained full control of her trust…. Approximately thirty million."

I leaned back in my chair and stared at him.

"Who the heck was her mother?" Kate asked, slowly shaking her head.

"Jessica. I was her second husband. Her first husband was Henry Morton."

"The media tycoon," I said.

He nodded. "Yes. When he died in that airplane crash, she inherited everything. She sold it all soon after she married me. And then we had the children, so she set up trust funds for their educations and futures. Ten million each. Wise investing increased that over the years until... well, you understand, I'm sure."

I sure as hell do.

"Okay, so what *does* happen to her money?"

"The way Jessica set it up was that if anything happened to one or more of the children, the survivors would benefit. It will go to my two sons, split equally between them; they'll each get approximately 14.5 million."

Hah! And there's the motive.

He caught my look. "No... no, they wouldn't."

"Stranger things, Mr. Martan. Who else would benefit from her death? How about your other son, Caspian?"

"No. He is mine and Vivien's child."

"How about you, sir?"

He smiled, for the first time since we'd met. "No," he said. "Mr. Starke. Do you have any idea how much I'm worth?" He didn't wait for an answer. "If you did, you'd know that a paltry few million dollars wouldn't even be a drop in the proverbial bucket."

"She was engaged to be married, correct?"

"Yes, to Sebastian Carriere. He's a local man, of Caribbean descent."

"You mean he's black," Kate said bluntly.

He rolled his eyes. "Yes, he's black. So what?"

"Not a thing," Kate said. "Just clarifying things. How did you feel about that, about your daughter marrying—" she made air quotes with her fingers "—'a man of Caribbean descent'?"

He shrugged. "That's a loaded question, Lieutenant."

"Which is why I asked it. How did you feel?"

"She was her own woman. Had been for a very long time. My feelings were irrelevant."

"So tell us about him," I said.

He nodded. "He owns a charter fishing boat. Stays busy, most of the time. He's likable enough, but she could have done better—but all fathers think that of their daughters, don't they?"

"They get along okay?" she asked.

"As far as I know, yes. He spent most of his days on the water. Came up here on Sundays for dinner. Other than that, he was rarely here."

"Was he here yesterday?" I asked.

"I don't think so. He could have been, but if he was, I didn't see him. I know he was here on Friday evening, and that they'd also been arguing; about what, I don't know."

I nodded. "Do you think she actually intended to marry him?"

"Yes, of course. Why do you ask?"

"A condom wrapper was found under her bed," I said, watching him closely. "We know she was using a contraceptive device, so why the condom? Carriere would not have used one, so that means…."

He looked shocked, or at least he tried to. His mouth opened and closed again and then, shaking his head, he said, "No, no, absolutely not. You're saying she was… oh no. That was not happening." And I almost believed that he believed it.

"So," I said thoughtfully, watching his eyes. "Hypothetically, let's say she *was* having an affair. The question is with whom. It had to be someone in this house, family or staff. Who would be your best guess?"

"No one…. Hell! No one. *Family*? That's disgusting. I can't think of anyone…." And there it was, just a slight twitch of his right eyelid as he glanced away. It was fleeting, and he came right back to hold my gaze, but it was enough. I looked at Kate. She was tapping away on her iPad, but she also had a half smile on her lips.

Yeah, we know, don't we?

I decided to let it go for now. I looked at my watch. The thirty minutes were up, and I had a whole lot more I would have liked to have asked him, but it could wait. This was, after all, his party.

"Okay, Mr. Martan," I said, getting up from behind the desk. "That's enough for now. If you wouldn't mind sending Leo in next, please; we'll talk to you again later today. This afternoon, perhaps."

"So," I said to Kate as the door closed behind him. "What do you think?"

"Same as you. She was screwing someone and he has a good idea who; we need to figure it out. Let's face it; there aren't many candidates. At the moment, I can think of only three... no, four."

I nodded. "Michael Collins, Jeffery Margolis, Moore, and Jackson, right?"

"Yep. Them. We also need to talk to Sebastian, and soon. For now, though, I'm looking forward to our chat with Leo Jr."

So am I.

Chapter 8

Leo Jr. had all the finesse of a Cat D6 bulldozer. He came into the office loaded for bear and ready for a fight.

He was about the same height as his father, but there the resemblance ended. Where the elder man was trim and fit, Junior was overweight and in dire need of exercise. His face had the florid look of a drinker. At some point in his life he'd suffered a broken nose, and his neck was a field of old acne scars. His hair, already receding, was combed over in a vain attempt to cover the suntanned expanse of his forehead. His clothes were casual but expensive: the tan pants were perfectly pressed, though his paunch hung over his belt, and the sleeves of his blue sport shirt were rolled perfectly up to just above the elbow— more I think to show off the gold, diamond-encrusted Rolex than for comfort. He wore no socks with his Ferragamo boat loafers. He was, in fact, the epitome of the preppy young man about the yacht club, only at thirty-three he wasn't so young.

No, Leo was everything most people hate about the privileged class. He wore his money ostentatiously; his clothes were his badge of honor and position.

And he'll fill those damned expensive pants when he finds out what I know about him.

93

"Sit down, Mr. Martan," I said sarcastically as he slumped down into the chair in front of the desk, iPhone in hand. "You won't need that. Please turn it off until we're done."

"Uh… no!" He said it lightly and with a twisted smirk. "I'll keep it on if you don't mind. I may need something to occupy my mind while you drone on."

I nodded and smiled sweetly at him. "Make the most of it, sonny. They don't allow them in prison."

That got his attention. "What?"

"That's what happens to people like you. Does your father know the mess you're in?"

"I… I don't know what the hell you're talking about."

"Yeah you do. You're broke, Leo. Not only that, you're being investigated for investment fraud. What's the name of the fund you're operating…?" I spread my papers—the hard copies that Tim had supplied—out across the desk and looked at each one in turn. "Ah yes. Here it is. Brighton New Horizon. You truly did screw those old folks over, didn't you? Twenty-one million dollars and change. And now the FBI's coming for you."

The color drained from his face. His bottom lip trembled. He wrung the iPhone in his hands like a dish towel.

"It's not what you think. It was just some unfortunate investments."

"That's not what it says here," I said, picking up one of the sheets of paper and waving it at him. "You're running a full-blown Ponzi scheme. You're taking in cash from retirees, and you're stealing it. The fund is in the hole for twenty-one million. The fourteen or fifteen million you hope to get from Gabrielle's trust fund will plug the hole, at least for a little while, but you're going down."

I looked him up and down, shook my head, and smiled. "And oh boy are you going down. Do you have any idea what happens to people like you when they go to prison? Of course you don't. But I digress. That money represents motive. You killed your sister to get your hands on it, didn't you?"

The iPhone fell from his fingers as he jumped to his feet. "Screw you!" he yelled as he picked it up. "You're out of your goddamn mind. I loved my sister!"

"Sit down," I said quietly. "If you don't, I'll have Tommy Quinn arrest you." *Where the hell is Quinn, I wonder? He should have been back with Carriere by now.*

Slowly, Leo Jr. lowered himself back into his chair.

"Now, Lieutenant," I said to Kate. "Why don't you take this? I'm having trouble even looking at this piece of garbage."

"You were arguing with Gabrielle early yesterday morning, just before she was murdered," Kate said. "What was that about?"

"Money, of course, and I wasn't the only one she argued with that morning. I heard her screaming across the balconies at someone in the Margolises' suite too."

I made a note of that, and then asked him again what he was arguing with her about.

"I asked her to lend me some money to pay into the fund, but *not* because I was stealing from it. I made some bad investments and—"

"Yes, I see that you did," Kate said. "A Lamborghini Aventador: four hundred thousand; a Maserati Convertible with all the trimmings: two hundred thousand; and then there's the helicopter, a Bell 407—" she looked up at him "—over two and a half million, and there's more. You've been living high off the hog, Mr. Martan, haven't you?"

"It's not like that."

Kate raised her eyebrows. "Really? Do tell."

"The helicopter I got used for just under two mill, and I need it to get back and forth to the office in Miami. Living here is… well you… hell, it's not easy to get in and out. I need it."

"And the cars?"

"Image. It's all about image, perception. Who the hell will invest with a guy driving a damned Volkswagen, for God's sake?"

Well, he does have a point, sort of. Good answer, Leo.

"So you were arguing about money," Kate continued. "Tell us about that."

"There's nothing to tell; I wanted to borrow ten million from her and she wouldn't give it to me."

"How could she? She didn't have it yet."

"She could have borrowed it against her inheritance. It would only have been for a few weeks. Look, I didn't kill her. She was a pain in the ass sometimes, but she was my little sister. I *loved* her, and I want to see her killer caught, I really do, but it wasn't me." He looked as if he were about to cry.

Damn it if I don't halfway believe you, I thought.

"Okay, Leo," I said. One more thing and then you can go. Where were you between noon and two o'clock yesterday?"

"That's easy. I was out sailing. I have a small Sunfish. I was out most of the afternoon."

Just as his old man said.

"Okay. You can go, but don't leave the island. I know damned well we're going to want to talk to you again."

He rose slowly to his feet, stuffing the phone into his pocket with one hand and wiping his eyes with the other. His shoulders were slumped, his head down. When he got to the door he turned and, shaking his head, said again, tearfully, "I didn't do it."

Chapter 9

Leo Jr.'s wife was something of an anomaly. We'd decided to see her next in light of our interview with her husband.

Leo was thirty-six; Lucy was twenty-six, and she was his second wife. She'd once had money. Not a lot compared to the Martans, but significant. A trophy wife? She was indeed a beautiful woman, and intelligent, which made me wonder what the hell she saw in Leo. Position and status, perhaps? I thought so. I was eminently familiar with people like her, living on Lookout Mountain as I did. Maybe he saw her as an investment, a source of new funding. We were about to find out.

I say she was beautiful, and she was, but not like some of the blonde Barbies we see on television these days. No, this one was a classic, dark-haired, dark-skinned beauty; tall, slender, with sharp features and full lips. Aristocratic. Hispanic? Maybe. She was dressed in workout gear: sports bra, spandex pants, and Nike running shoes. And she obviously spent a lot of time in the gym because she was also in great shape. *That six-pack would be the envy of many a pro wrestler.*

"You look as if you've just come from the gym," I said as she walked in and took her seat.

"I've just come back from a run around the golf course. I need a shower in the worst way."

Now that did set me back a little. First, she didn't look to me as if she needed a shower at all, and second, I run myself, two, three miles most mornings—but over the golf course, and in this heat?

"Impressive," I said. "That has to be... what, four miles?"

"It's more like five, actually." She had a slight smile on her lips, but there was no humor in it. Like everyone else, she'd rather be anywhere but seated in front of me.

I looked sideways at Kate. Obviously not as impressed as me, she had her head tilted down slightly and was staring at Lucy with a half smile on her lips. Then she looked up, reached across the desk, picked up a piece of paper and a pen, wrote something on the paper, and slid it over to me.

I smiled when I read it.

Stop it! You're a married man now.

I looked at her and winked; she didn't find it funny. She leaned back in her chair and said, "So, Mrs. Martan. If you didn't kill Gabrielle, who did?"

Okay. I see what you're doing, I thought. *Shock and awe. Nice one, Kate.*

Unfortunately, if it had any effect on Lucy, she didn't show it. She simply leaned back in her chair, folded her arms, exposed her amazing six pack, and smiled—first at Kate, then at me.

"Is that what you think? That I killed Gabby? Leo, my husband, said you were a couple of rubes from the hills of Tennessee. I'm beginning to think he might be right."

I gave her a big, toothy grin, my best impression of a redneck, and replied, "As ever was, missy. As ever was."

Kate, however, didn't find it so funny, "Yeah that husband of yours is a real pistol. He'll make someone a fine wife when he goes down on a federal rap for fraud."

Lucy glared at Kate, and started to rise to her feet to leave.

"Sit down, Mrs. Martan," I said. "You only got as good as you gave. So let's get started, shall we? I'd like you to account for your whereabouts between noon and two o'clock yesterday."

"I was at the stables with my horses from... oh, I don't know; around ten until just after one, and then I came up here for a late lunch. Then I went to the pool. I was there until I heard the noise."

Stables? They have stables too?

"What noise was that?"

"Oh, there was a whole lot of yelling and screaming, most it from Vivien, when they found Gabrielle."

"Did anyone see you?" Kate asked.

She shrugged. "Can anyone confirm my alibi, you mean? I'm sure someone did see me, but I didn't take notes. The servants are not... well, they're servants, and I have as little to do with them as possible."

Wow. What a bitch.

Kate stared at her. She didn't like Lucy one bit, and didn't bother to hide it.

"I need names, Mrs. Martan," she said. The hostile undertone in her voice might have chilled even me. "We need to confirm your alibi. Without it, you'll be in for a tough time until we can figure out who did this thing, and right now, you're a prime suspect."

"Oh don't be ridiculous," she snapped. "Why on earth would I want to kill my husband's sister?"

"Money," Kate snapped back. "Your husband's broke and under federal investigation. With Gabrielle dead, her inheritance goes to her brothers. That would be about fifteen million each for him and Evander. That's motive enough for you and for him. So, tell me. Account for your time between noon and two. Give me some names."

"I can't. I told you. I didn't see anyone. Well I did, but I can't remember who. You'll have to ask around... oh, wait. I saw Caspian. He came to the pool just as I was leaving."

"That's not an alibi." Kate shook her head, exasperated. "That only proves you were there at two o'clock. You could have arrived there at 1:55, for Christ's sake. You'll have to do a whole lot better than that."

"Well I can't. As I said, you'll just have to ask around...." She paused, looked first at Kate, then at me, and then said, quietly, "You do know she was screwing Jeff Margolis, don't you?

The silence was deafening. The shock of what she said was complete.

"Is that a fact," I said quietly. "Why don't you tell me about it?"

"What's to tell? They'd been at it for months. Everyone knew—except Leo's father, that is. To the rest of us it was a huge joke. There was talk that she was screwing the butler too, and I wouldn't have been surprised if she'd been doing Mike Collins as well. She loved her nookie, that's for sure. You didn't know any of that, did you."

I should have been surprised, but I wasn't. Gabrielle had obviously been doing someone, of that I was certain and, upon thinking about it, it kinda made sense. She was right next door to Jeff's suite, but Collins? Moore? *And* Sebastian?

Hell, if it's true, she had herself quite a little poodle parlor going. I wonder if she was doing anyone else... Jackson, perhaps? Nah.... Hell, maybe she was.

"I thought not," she said. "Now you have something better to think about, don't you?" She sighed, softened a little, looked first at Kate and then at me.

"Look," she continued. "Gabrielle was an expensive little piece of trash, a slut that would screw anything with a…. So she pissed off everyone in the house? So just about everyone hated her? So she was screwing Jeff for sure, and maybe the butler, and probably Jackson and Michael too? So someone lost their temper and hit her over the head with a bottle? Does that *surprise* you, for God's sake? Family, staff, our friends; she wasn't in the least particular. And she was an arrogant little bitch. I'm only surprised that someone didn't do it years ago. I didn't do it, but there were times I wanted to." She paused for breath, then continued, "I was there one time when Leo, my husband, begged her to help him out. She could have gotten him the money he needed, but instead she taunted him. Look, I didn't like her. I don't think anyone did, not even that exotic fiancé of hers. If I had to guess who did it…. I couldn't. It could have been any one of them, really."

She was right. We did now have plenty to think about. In fact, she'd just thrown half a dozen wrenches into the gears. If what she said was true….

"So," she said. "If you're done, I need to leave. As I said, I need a shower, and I have the

104

horses to see to." She rose to her feet. This time I didn't stop her. She closed the door behind her and I turned to Kate.

"Well," I said, switching off the recorder. "What do you think about that?"

"I think if even a tiny piece of what she said is true, our little Gabby was quite the piece of work."

"And?" I prompted.

"What do I think about Lucy Martan? You already know what I think. She's a first-class rich bitch, but did she do it? Maybe, maybe not. I'd say she has it in her all right, maybe in the heat of the moment she lost her temper, but I don't think so. I mean, she's so self-centered, wrapped up in her own little world. It's all about her. Everything is about her."

"And that in itself is motive," I said. "She needs to protect and maintain her status. If her husband goes to jail she'll become an outcast. The money would stave that off for a while maybe, but unless they can come up with another ten million, and quickly, he's going to jail. Now he has her inheritance they can borrow against. They, both of them, are desperate. She might not show it, but I guarantee that she is. And desperate people do desperate things, including murder...."

"Nope. Sorry. I still think the butler did it, and now that we know he was screwing the victim...."

"Yeah, right... the butler. If I didn't know you were joking.... Kate, we don't know that she was screwing him. We only have Lucy's word for that. In fact, we only have her word that Gabby was screwing anyone other than her fiancé. Everything she said might be nothing more than a smokescreen."

"Could be," Kate said, "but somehow I don't think so. I think there was more to Gabby than meets the eye, a whole lot more, and we need to find out exactly what it—what *she* was. So who's next on the list?"

"That would be Evander Martan, but...." I looked at my watch. "It's almost noon, and that woman has left a nasty taste in my mouth. We need to get lunch. I wonder if they have anything here."

They did. It was something even I had not come across before, not even on the exalted heights of Lookout Mountain. The dining-room table had been laid out buffet-style with a meal fit for the gods: conch salad, conch fritters, smoked salmon, crab cakes, stuffed chicken Normandy, fried lobster tail, Seafood Newburg; there was even a carving station with a chef handing out roast turkey, roast beef, and, the pièce de résistance, cold roast pheasant. Where the hell that had come from, and at what cost, I had no idea. I tell you, I've been to some fancy lunches, but that one had them all beat.

I got myself a plate—well, a platter—loaded it up, and went into the conservatory to call Amanda. She took the call poolside, asked me how it was going, told me she missed me and couldn't wait until dinner to see me. Nice, but I felt kinda dismal; it was, after all, only my second day of married life. *What a hell of a way to spend a honeymoon.*

I disconnected and sat there by myself picking at an assortment of conch, crab, pheasant, lobster.... *Oh hell, I'm going to regret this later.*

I set the plate aside, cradled a pint of icy pink lemonade between my palms, and stared out the picture window at a view that money just couldn't buy: the rolling fairways and the ocean just beyond. *I've got to try to find time to get the old man out on the course. It's beautiful....*

It was at that point that the door opened, and Tommy Quinn stuck his head inside.

"Sorry to interrupt your lunch, but we have Carriere outside. What do you want us to do with him?"

"Bring him in; I'll see him right after Moore. Where was he?"

"He was out on his boat. Fishing charter. We grabbed him as soon as he docked. He ain't a happy man."

"Okay. Give me fifteen minutes with Moore, and then let's have him in Leo's office. And... well, we need to get the fingerprinting

107

done. Now that everyone's here, can you get that started?"

"Yes, of course. If they're all here it shouldn't take more than an hour. What do you want me to do with the scans when I'm finished?"

"You need to get with Ms. Patel and have her send you her scans of the latent prints from the scene, and then get both sets to Tim. He'll process everything and run comparisons. That good?"

He nodded. "Sounds like a plan. I'll get right on it."

I took a bathroom break, did what needed to be done, then washed my hands and face in icy water and headed back out for what I was sure would be another confrontational interview.

Chapter 10

Victor Moore didn't seem surprised when I found him in the dining room and asked him to accompany me to Leo Martan's office. In fact, I got the distinct impression he was expecting it.

Even sitting in front of the desk, he looked uncomfortable. I watched him. He looked at me, and then quickly looked away. He looked at Kate; same reaction.

"Is something wrong, Mr. Moore?" I asked.

"No," he answered, just a little too sharply. "I'm simply wondering why I'm here."

"You're here," I said, "because the word is that you were having an affair with Gabrielle Martan. Were you?"

He smiled. "Is that what they're saying. I'm not surprised. No. I wasn't having an affair with her."

"So tell us. What was your relationship with Ms. Gabrielle?" I asked.

"I was... her protector? I don't know. I've been here, with Mr. Martan, for more than eighteen years. She was only seven then. I've looked after the family all that time. We were close, in a way. It's hard to explain: not brotherly; certainly not romantically. I was very fond of her.... No, I loved her. Oh, not like that," he said when he saw the look Kate was giving him. "Look, I was more of a father to that kid than Martan ever was. He never had time for her. I always did. She could, and did, come to me with all her little problems, when she was a little girl and even as she grew up. She was a bit loose, but she was also a product of her times, school, and upbringing."

"Loose?" Kate asked. "What do you mean by that?"

"I know you've talked to Mr. Martan Jr., and his... wife." He almost spit the word out. "But she was a good girl, and anyone who says different will answer to me."

"It's said that she was having an affair with Jeffery Margolis," Kate said. "Did you know about that?" He did. I caught the twitch of his upper lip.

"Bullshit," he snapped.

I nodded. *No it wasn't.*

"Where were you between noon and two o'clock yesterday, Mr. Moore?"

"Hah! You think *I* killed her?" He was incredulous. "You're out of your minds, both of you. I was here in the house. All over the damned place, as always. I'm the most visible person on the property."

"Oh, that's for sure," I said, "which also means that no one takes a lot of notice of your comings and goings. Ten minutes; five, even.

That's all would have taken to hit her over the head and toss her off the balcony."

The look he gave me was one a tiger would have been proud of. He stood, walked quickly to the door and, without a backward look, left the office, slamming the door behind him.

"He's either terribly naïve," Kate said, "or just didn't want to see what was going on right under his nose. I'm inclined to believe the latter. I think he knew, but couldn't accept it and simply looked the other way."

"Oh he knew all right," I said. "The question still is: Was he screwing her too?"

Chapter 11

Sebastian Carriere was in every sense a man of the Islands, and by that I mean he was possessed of a somewhat biting sense of humor—developed, I imagined, over long years of dealing with the public, and not just the rich and famous. He was a handsome man: thirty-five, aristocratic, carried himself stiffly upright, perhaps to compensate for his lack of stature. He was five foot ten, maybe a little more, but what he lacked in height he more than made up for in attitude, and despite what Leo Martan had said, he was more Hispanic than African American; in fact, he reminded me of a bull fighter, slim, arrogant, long black hair, shiny and slicked straight back and tied in a ponytail, dark eyes, clean shaven. He was the quintessential romance novel cover model. He looked like he'd stepped out of another age. In short, they don't make 'em like that anymore. I could see why Gabrielle had been attracted to him, as were a great many more members of the fairer sex, I had no doubt.

"You were supposed to be here this morning. Your fiancée has been murdered, for God's sake. Where the hell have you been?" I asked as he sat down.

He shrugged and wrinkled his nose. "On my boat. I have a business to run. I don't work; I don't pay my bills; I lose my boat." The voice was refined, with little trace of his Caribbean origins.

This is one cold-hearted son of a bitch.

"You were heard arguing with Gabrielle on Friday evening. What was that about?"

"I asked her to lend me some money. She wouldn't. I was angry."

"Did you see her yesterday morning?"

"No. I was working."

"Where were you from noon until two?"

"I told you. I was working. I was at the boat dock, preparing the boat for my guests."

"What time did you cast off?"

He shrugged, thought for a moment, then said, "I'm not sure: two thirty, three. They were a rowdy bunch. I really wasn't paying that much attention."

"That late? Did no one tell you about Gabrielle? Did no one call you?"

"No and yes. No one came to the dock to tell me, and I keep my phone in a compartment by the wheel. I didn't hear it. They were very noisy; so are the engines. When I finally got to it there were several missed calls."

"You didn't check for messages?" Kate asked incredulously.

He shrugged again. It seemed to be some sort of conversational idiosyncrasy, and it was annoying.

"I was at sea," he said. "No signal. And anyway, everyone knows that I don't check my phone when I'm working. Running the boat takes all my attention. These are dangerous waters. Reefs everywhere. I wouldn't have answered even if I had heard it."

"So when did you learn of your fiancée's death?"

"Last night, when I returned from my charter. It was late. It was a moonlight party cruise. Ten people. They got very drunk. It was after eleven when I docked. I checked my phone and came straight here." He shrugged, expressively. "As to this morning: What could I do? I had an inshore charter already booked for eight o'clock, so I took them out. I need the money and they had already paid. Losing that money would not have brought her back."

"But you knew you were supposed to meet with us this morning, did you not?"

Again the shrug, this time with a shake of his head. "I knew, and I also knew that you would be here all day. And why talk to me anyway? I was not here when she died. Again I say I have a business to run."

"Where are you from, Mr. Carriere? Your accent is… different?"

"Why? Is it important?"

"Not at all. I'm just curious."

"I am from Cuba." He pronounced it "Kooba." "My family maintains that we are descended from the Spanish pirate Juan Garcia."

And I have no doubt that you are, I thought. "Let's go back to Friday evening. You say you were arguing about money, that you wanted her to give you some. How much were you asking for?"

"Not give, lend. I asked her for five thousand. She refused."

Jeez. Is that all? That's not a motive.

"Nothing else?" Kate asked pointedly.

"Like what?"

"Like the affair she was having with Jeffery Margolis."

He didn't flinch. He shrugged, looked down at the floor, and said, "Yes. I mean, no. I knew about that, but there was nothing to it. She was that way, promiscuous, but it didn't mean anything, and she had promised me it was over."

"When was that?" Kate asked.

"I don't know. Two, three weeks ago. I didn't make a note of the date," he said sarcastically.

"So who else do you think might have been screwing her?" Kate stared intently at him.

His eyes narrowed and his lips tightened as he glared back at her. "Why do you ask that?"

115

"Because we found a condom wrapper under her bed."

"That would have been mine," he said with a slight smile. "I think I left it on the nightstand on Friday evening."

"Yours?" I asked incredulously. "But you were engaged to her... and she was wearing a contraceptive patch. Why would you use a condom?"

Again the shrug. "I have a bit of a problem," he said, without rancor. "I am HIV positive. I always used one, to protect her." I looked sideways at Kate. She was as stunned as I was.

"But the patch...."

He interrupted me. "That was not for me, my friend. I told you she was promiscuous. Evidently she was still screwing Jeff... or maybe someone else." He had a wry smile on his face.

Yup. He's one cold SOB.

I shook my head, exasperated. I'd had just about enough for one day. This guy was an enigma. His wife-to-be had been screwing around on him and he didn't seem to care.

"You're telling me you knew your fiancée was playing the field and you didn't care? What the hell kind of man are you?"

He sat up straight in the chair, his shoulders rigid, his head held high.

Oh yes, he's a pirate all right.

116

"I am the kind of man who was unfortunate enough to receive a blood transfusion on one of the more remote islands. The blood was bad. I contracted the virus. Gabrielle and I, we loved each other. We could not, however, enjoy a normal sex life. While she catered to my needs as best she could, she had needs of her own; needs I could not properly fulfill, and so she... she... she... went with other men. I didn't like it, nor did I condone it, but what was I to do? Give her up? No, my friend. That I would never do.

"I will tell you something else," he continued. "You had better find out who did do this thing, because if you don't, I will, and the consequences will not be pretty; by my ancestors I promise you that. Now, if you're done with me, I have a charter to fulfill."

It was quite a speech, and I had to admit, I was impressed, and so, I could see, was Kate.

"Just a couple more questions, Mr. Carriere, and then you can go. You say the condom wrapper was yours, that you left it on the nightstand. It was found yesterday morning under the bed, after the room had been cleaned. How do you explain that if you were not in her room that morning?"

He shrugged. It was really beginning to get on my nerves.

"The cleaner must have missed it. That is the only explanation there could be, no?"

I nodded, flipped back through my notes. "Gabrielle was killed sometime between twelve and two yesterday afternoon. You said you were at the dock, preparing for your charter. Did anyone see you there during those hours, anyone who might confirm your presence there?"

He shrugged. Again. "Perhaps, perhaps not. You must check for yourself."

I nodded. "That you can count on. You're not planning on leaving the island, are you? Because if you are, don't. We'll need to talk to you again. Oh, and keep your phone where you can hear it."

He stood, went to the door, opened it, then turned and said, "Good bye, Mr. Starke, and good hunting."

"Well," Kate said, after the door had closed behind him, "that opens a whole new line of investigation. As far as we know, she could have been screwing any one or all of them, her brothers exclu... ded. Oh no, not them, surely?"

"Yes, you're right, but what did you think of him?" I asked her.

"I liked him. He *could* have killed her, but I don't think so."

"How about you, Bob?" I asked. He and Quinn, having made short work of the finger printing, had joined us after Moore had left the office.

He shrugged, and was about to speak when Kate interrupted him. "Oh for Christ's sake, don't you start with the shrugs."

He grinned at her, shrugged again, this time deliberately, and said, "I don't know what to make of him. He didn't seem too bothered that his fiancée had just been murdered. I say we need to keep an eye him, and check around the docks, see if he really was there yesterday. Someone should have seen him. It's busy down there most of the time. I like him too. He has a big problem with his health and I think he's handling it as best he can. I can't imagine… well, you know."

I did know. I also knew I'd had enough for one day. I looked at my watch. It was almost one thirty. I needed to spend some time with my family. I also needed time to think.

"Okay, people. I've had it. We still need to interview Vivien, Evander, Caspian, the Margolises, the gardener…." I looked at my list. "The Collinses, and Georgina. Jesus, we've barely scratched the surface…. Nope. I'm not doing any more of this today." I looked over at Tommy and smiled.

"But you, Tommy, you're at work. You're being paid to do this, so I want you to continue conducting interviews. You can do Georgina Walford, Caspian Martan, and the two Collinses this afternoon. You can leave Alicia and Jeffery Margolis, Evander Martan, and Vivien to Kate and me. We'll get to them in the morning. I'll meet you at my cottage at the resort at eight in the morning, and we'll go over your interviews. Sound good?"

He looked kind of put out, but he agreed.

"Kate," I said, "if you would call our group and set them up for ten o'clock tomorrow morning, I'll let Leo Sr. know what we're doing. He won't be pleased, but screw him."

I was right. He wasn't pleased, and he did his best to talk me out of it. But eventually he agreed to run us back to the resort and to meet with us when we arrived back at the Mount the following morning. He also tried his best to find out where I was with the investigation, but I wasn't having any of that either. I didn't know anything, and I wouldn't have told him if I did.

Chapter 12

Leo drove Kate, Bob, and me back to the resort and we went our separate ways; me to grab a shower, Kate and Bob to do whatever. We arranged to meet for dinner at eight. The rest of the day was mine, all mine... and Amanda's, and by God if I had to throw away my iPhone to get some peace, I'd do it.

I'd called her just before I went to close out the day with Leo, and she was waiting for me when I got back to the cottage. She looked fantastic in a white bikini and an almost transparent, red-and-white flowered beach cover. I went to grab her, but she was having none of it.

"Not right now," she said, backing away. "I've arranged something special, and they're waiting for us. So do what you have to; get changed, and let's go."

"Whoa. Wait just a minute. I don't want to be around anyone but you, and I need to talk to Tim before I do anything. So cancel whatever it is you've arranged."

"Nope. You'll like this. I know you will. Tim and Sammie are outside on the patio. So strip; get into swim gear and a shirt. Take five to talk to Tim, and then we're away to the dock."

"Damn, damn, damn," I mumbled as I headed to the bedroom. "Is this how it's going to be? I hate people making me—"

"I can hear you!"

Still grumbling to myself, I did as she'd asked. I changed into a pair of Tommy Bahama swim trunks and a loose-fitting white linen shirt and headed out to find Tim. He and Sammie were indeed on the patio, he with an incongruous white shield covering his nose, Sammie looking very fetching in a black one piece.

"Hey," I said as I dragged out a chair and joined them at the table. "I need a quick word."

"You got it," Tim said.

"Did Tommy Quinn give you the fingerprint scans?"

"Yep. He sent the files to me. I was going to run comparisons this afternoon. Is that okay?"

"Yes, fine. Amanda and I are heading out; for how long, I have no idea, but it would be nice if you could have that ready for us by morning. Can you do that?"

"Sure. No problem. I already have the basic CSIpix Matcher fingerprint comparator software in the Cloud. I can use that, and everything else I need is on my laptop, or back at the office, which I'm connected to via Wi-Fi. Anyway, if we're just comparing local images— family and staff—I have what I need. I'll just transfer everything from Daisy and Lieutenant

Quinn's files to my computer and away we go. If I need to get into AFIS, however…. Well, I can do it, but it will take a little time."

"You can get into the national AFIS database?" I asked, stunned at the very idea.

"Um… uh, no," he said, sheepishly. "Of course, not. Well, not officially."

Oh hell. The boy's going to end up in jail, and me along with him.

"Do *not*," I said, as sternly as I could, which wasn't easy, considering the wounded-puppy look he was giving me. "Do *not* do that *ever* again. Do you understand?"

He nodded.

"We'll get Kate to do it, okay?"

He nodded again, this time grinning.

"In the meantime, this CSI software you have—and I don't like the sound of that either—it will do what we need?"

"Oh yeah, and it's a private proprietary software—CSIpix is a legitimate company. You bought the software for me a few months ago for—"

"I did?"

"Well, you didn't. I did. It only cost, like, six hundred, so…."

"Tim, why do you *never* ask me when you want something? Why do you just go ahead and get it?"

"Well you're always so busy! And six hundred's not a lot, not for this kind of tech."

"From now on, you *ask*, damn it... still, I'm glad you have it. If it will do what we need, that is."

"Oh, it will, so long as I don't need to get into AFIS—"

"*Stop*. I said no more AFIS, and I meant it. Now, I need to get the hell out of here before I pull a Donald on you and fire your ass."

I didn't miss the sly grin he gave me as I got up and shoved back my chair. I leaned over, put both hands flat on the tabletop in front of him, leaned in close, and whispered loudly enough for them both to hear, "Log into AFIS one more time and I swear...."

The grin never left his face. *Damn it. The boy knows me far too well.*

"Have a nice time, boss."

I shook my head and left them to it.

Ten minutes later Amanda and I were at the dock, and she was right. The moment I saw the *Lady May* I fell in love with her. She was a forty-four-foot Lagoon 440 catamaran sailboat, the most beautiful boat I'd ever seen.

"Well?" Amanda asked. "Did I do good or what?"

"Depends. I hope there's someone to sail her."

"Of course there is, silly. Come and meet Captain Walker and Tag."

And what a pair they were.

Walker was a Barbados native in his early thirties, a tall black man with a shaved head and an overwhelming sense of humor. He liked to talk, constantly, but I took to him immediately. He wore only a pair of raggedy cargo shorts, and sported a set of muscles that had to be seen to be believed. Tag, however, was something else altogether. She too was a Barbadian, tall, slim, with skin the color of coffee grounds and a huge halo of black hair. She was maybe twenty-five and dressed in cut-off jeans she could only have gotten into with the aid of a shoehorn, and a scarlet bikini top. She was beautiful, quiet, and graceful.

"Welcome to the *Lady May*," Walker said, with a smile that stretched from ear to ear. He reached out, grabbed my hand, and shook it vigorously. "Let's get aboard. We got a long way to go."

"Keep your eyes in your head, Harry," Amanda whispered as we followed them up onto the boat.

I slipped my arm around her waist and whispered in her ear, "I have eyes only for you."

"If that's true, boy did you ever change," she whispered back.

"Not fair," I said, taking her hand and steadying her as she stepped onto the boat.

"What would you like to drink?" Tag asked, as Amanda and I took our seats at the rear of the well.

"I don't suppose you have any—"

"Laphroaig?" she asked, and without waiting for an answer, went on, "Of course. Mrs. Starke provided a bottle." There it was again: "Mrs. Starke." It was a little unnerving, but I was beginning to get used to it, and I liked it.

"Just a small one for now please, Tag. What do you and Captain Walker have planned for us this afternoon?"

"We gonna cruise to Black Rock at Salt Island in the BVI," she replied, "for some snorkeling over the wreck of the *RMS Rhone*. She sank in a hurricane in 1867. The stern section of the ship, what's left of it, lies between fifteen to thirty-five feet underwater. The rest of the wreck is much deeper. The water is crystal clear. You'll love it. Then we'll have a bite to eat. You can get some sun, take it easy in the guest suite as we sail back, if you want—" she looked slyly at Amanda as she said that last bit "—and we'll be back on Calypso Key by about 7:15. Does that sound good?"

It did, and we settled ourselves down to watch as they made the boat ready to leave. In less than ten minutes we were heading northeast

126

at a fine clip. It was one of those magical days. The sky was blue, dotted here and there with fluffy white clouds, and the sun shone down on the *Lady May* as she cut through the calm water that gurgled along the twin hulls, talking to us, singing a song I couldn't understand but that was strangely hypnotic nonetheless.

Amanda had stripped off her beach cover and was stretched out on one of the trampolines up front. The sun was high, but she already had a tan and was lathered in sunscreen, so she was in little danger of burning. Me? I had a tan too, but mine was a five or ten minute a day thing, and I figured no amount of sunscreen would save me from the ravages of Mr. Sol. That being so, I had seated myself under the awning on the forward bridge and, with the small shot of Laphroaig now nothing more than a memory, was sipping on a very tall, very cold Yellow Bird.

With the boat under full sail, she fairly flew over what few waves there were. We'd been out for no more than twenty minutes when I heard Amanda squeal.

"What the hell?" I asked Walker, jumping up, trying to see what was wrong.

"It's arl right," he said, grinning. "It's just dolphins she's spotted."

"Harry, Harry, c'mere, quickly."

I set my drink down in the cup holder and made my way unsteadily forward, hanging on to any rope or cable I could catch hold of.

She was on her knees at the front of the trampoline, hanging over, looking down into the water. She looked around, saw me coming, and gestured for me to join her. More than a little unhappy about it, I carefully inched my way onto the trampoline and knelt down beside her.

"Look," she said, pointing first here, then there, then back again. At first all I could see was the water rushing by under the boat and for a minute it made my head spin, but then I saw them. There were at least six bottlenose dolphins under and in front of the boat, keeping pace with it, surging up and down, sweeping from side to side. Occasionally one would break the surface, its great gray back there one second and gone the next. Amanda was entranced and, yep, I admit it; I was too. And then they were gone.

For maybe five minutes we waited, staring down into the rushing water, but the show was over, and I reluctantly rolled over onto my back and gazed up into a perfect blue and white sky, and then at the bulging foresail straining and creaking under the pressure of an eight-knot breeze. I didn't want the moment to end, ever.

Amanda must have been able to sense my feelings, because she too rolled over, her chest against mine, her cheek next to mine, and then she slid her arms around my neck, and for the

128

next thirty minutes we just lay there, enjoying the moment; life was indeed good.

Except.... *Oh hell. I can already feel my back burning.*

It was just after three thirty that afternoon when Tag dropped anchor off Black Rock Point on the west side of Salt Island, and we weren't alone. There were at least a dozen other boats of various types and sizes at anchor.

"Don't worry," Watson said with a grin. For a moment, I thought he was going to finish the iconic piece of advice and tell us to be happy, but he didn't.

"This is one of the best scuba diving sites in arl the Caribbean," he said instead, opening a locker and taking out several sets of masks, flippers, and snorkels. "But we're goin' snarkellin'. You can both swim, I take it?" He didn't bother to wait for an answer. "Have you snarkeled before? You have. That's good. You know what to do then.

"I've set her close to the stern of the wreck where the water's shallow—well, I say shallow. It's fifteen feet or so at best, but the water's clear, there's plenty to see, and if you're adventurous you can make it down to the wreck easy enough. Most of them people is scuba divin' in deeper water, so we won't be runnin' into them. Here, put these on while I'm talkin'." He handed us each a set of gear and he and Tag set about putting on their own. "Tag and me, we're gonna take you over the wreck and show you the sights. Okay?"

We both nodded.

"So," he continued, "let me tell you what we got here. This is some fine divin'. Did you ever see the movie *The Deep* with Jacqueline Bisset and Nick Nolte? No? Oh well. Never mind. Anyway, some of the underwater sequences were shot right here." He stood, wriggled his feet inside his flippers, and when he was comfortable he sat down again.

"Now then, it was on a dark day in October of 1867 when the *RMS Rhone* set her anchor off Peter Island just over there." He waved his hand in the general direction of the island and continued, "When the hurricane hit the islands, it descended upon them quick-like. So strong were the winds that the anchor wouldn't hold the ship, and she began to drift. The captain ordered that the line be cut. He figured he would make a run for the open sea. But the eye of the storm came in from the south and slammed the ship onto the rocks right where we are now, at Black Rock Point. She hit the reef and broke her back and went down in just a few minutes, so they say. All but 23 of the 146 souls on board perished. Some were recovered and are buried here on the island…." For a moment, he lapsed into silence, and then was soon back to his normal, cheery self.

"Ready? Good. Let's do it then. Oh. One more thing—well, several, really. Stay close to me and Tag. Don't touch anything. Stay off the wreck. There are big eels down there; don't touch them. Take off your jewelry. Rings too, Mrs. Starke. I know, I know, you only just got it, but shiny stuff catches the light underwater and glitters. A barracuda likes nothing better than to snap at fingers with glittery things on them.... Oh come now. It will be arl right. They don't like people, stay away from them... mostly. Put your things in here. I'll lock it up." And he did.

"Put some of this on the inside of the lens," he said, handing Amanda a bottle of baby shampoo. "It will stop it fogging up. Wash that stuff off when you get in the water. Are we ready? Good!" And he jumped to his feet, waddled to the stern, and slid easily into the water. Tag hung back, waiting. I helped Amanda into the water and then jumped in after her.

It was amazing. The water felt like warm silk on my skin. I looked around. The others were close to me; we were in a tight group.

"Take no notice of other divers and snarkelers," Walker shouted. "Stay with me; be careful; don't touch anything, especially the coral. Masks on? Now put your head under, take a look around, then tell me what you see."

I pulled the mask and snorkel down, breathed in through my nose so that mask gripped my face, and looked down. An impossible distance below, I could see the barnacle- and coral-encrusted structure, a tangle of ironwork,

131

plating, and cable that stretched away into the darkness as the water grew deeper. Almost directly below was a huge, coral-encrusted shaft.

I brought my head up out of the water. "Oh my God," I spluttered. "It's incredible."

"What you see down there," Walker said, "was once the rudder post of the *Rhone*. The tip is maybe thirty feet. You can make it easy enough. You want to try?"

I looked at Amanda. She nodded. I took her hand.

"Let's do it," I said, and we both took a deep breath, jackknifed, and headed slowly down into the silent world that once had been the *RMS Rhone*.

I grabbed hold of the post with one hand and pulled Amanda to me with the other. I slipped my arm around her waist and for a few seconds we gazed out at the fantastic underwater world. We paused long enough to take in what little we could see of the sprawling wreck: a giant propeller, parts of the great engine and gears, the massive propeller shaft, and the largely intact stern section of the ship. And then we had to return to the surface to take a breath.

"Oh my God," Amanda gasped. "It's so beautiful. Did you see the fish, all those beautiful colors? Let's do it again. C'mon." And she grabbed my hand, jackknifed, her flippers in the air, and down she went, hauling me after her.

Again we anchored ourselves to the rudder post… well, I did. She anchored herself to me, to my back, her arms wrapped around me.

Details of the wreck began to emerge. The ship was lying on its starboard side. The stern was almost intact but the hull had begun to collapse. Here and there, picked out by shafts of sunlight from the surface, I could see pieces of the wooden deck, the teak planks remarkably well preserved after nearly a hundred and fifty years underwater. And then Amanda grabbed my hand again and pulled, and once again we surfaced.

"Oh my God," she gasped, coughing as she took in water. "Oh my God. Have you ever seen anything like it? I'm going back." And again, she turned her tail to the sun and, with a flash of her white-clad bottom, disappeared in a flurry of water. I followed. Now it was my turn. I slipped my arms around her, spit out the snorkel, and nibbled her neck, her ears; she wriggled around to face me, clamped herself onto me, and together we rose once more to the surface.

We dove down maybe a half dozen more times. Each time we grew a little more adventurous, until finally we made it onto the deck, a fantastic, silent world of indescribable beauty: corals, anemones, tube sponges, and the fish—it was a work of art more than 140 years in the making. Over almost a century and a half, the *Rhone* had transformed herself from a ship into a reef, and had become home to a myriad of undersea life. The Caribbean lobster, the moray eel, turtles, and thousands of reef fish: gray angels, sergeant majors, triggers, spotted eagle rays, sting rays, yellowtail snappers, and a hundred more I couldn't possibly begin to name made up its resident population.

We didn't want to leave, but Walker and Tag were already making the boat ready. So, reluctantly, we climbed the ladder onto the stern.

"We'll be under way in a couple of minutes," Walker said. "There are heads—bathrooms—below. Why don't you take a shower and... maybe a nap?" he suggested slyly. "You can use the master suite. We won't disturb you. We'll give you a shout when we're thirty minutes or so out from Calypso."

I looked at Amanda. She nodded, and that was what we did.

The cruise back to Calypso was one I'll never forget. The shower—we did it together—was another experience I'll never forget. By the time we made it in, the boat was under way and pitching slightly, tossing us back and forth against each other. It was a little disconcerting at first, but then we got the hang of it and the shower soon turned into something else entirely.

We never did get that nap, as Walker knew damn well we wouldn't, and boy did he look pleased with himself when we finally emerged from below.

"You two look like you need a drink!" he shouted down from the forward bridge. "Tag, look after the customers!"

And she did. A couple of minutes later, I was sipping on another Yellow Bird and Amanda on what could only have been a half pint of gin and tonic.

Dinner that Sunday evening was a quiet affair. Amanda and I were exhausted, and my arm was giving me a lot of grief from all the swimming. I looked down at the two scarlet scars—courtesy of Mr. Tree's partner, Kathryn Greene—and inwardly shuddered. Involuntarily, I rubbed the two wounds. The one on the inside, the entry wound, was quite small; the exit wound and surgical scars were something else. The surgeon had done an amazing job repairing the artery and pulling it all back together, but I was beginning to wonder if I would ever again be totally pain-free.

I felt a hand on my right arm. "Hey. Are you all right?" Amanda asked.

"Yeah. I'm fine." I wasn't, but what the hell. I took her hand, leaned over, and kissed her. "It hurts a little, is all, and I'm dreading leaving you again in the morning."

Chapter 13

A light breeze was blowing in off the ocean when we arrived at breakfast that next morning, and the temperature was a balmy seventy-three degrees. The tables were dressed with white linen cloths and small vases of colorful flowers: lilies, roses, hydrangea, and flax leaves.

Amanda had put on one of those little sundresses, and everyone else—except Dad and Rose, who were off hiking somewhere—was equally as comfortably dressed. I, for one, had on a pair of white linen pants and a pale blue, short-sleeved shirt. I also had my arm in a sling, a miniscule little thing that Amanda had made for me. Just enough to take the weight off my forearm. I hate those things, but she insisted.

The food—traditional US breakfast fare except for the Johnnycakes—was quickly dispensed with and the table cleared. It was time to get back to reality, at least for an hour or two.

"I've been thinking," I began, once everyone had refilled their coffee cups, "that this investigation is more than I want to fool with, especially here and now, but I made a promise, and I'll keep it, but on my... I should say *our* terms." I looked at Amanda. She shrugged, seemingly unconcerned.

"Hey, Tommy," I said as he walked up onto the patio. "Grab some coffee and take a seat. We were just about to get started."

He nodded, said hello to everyone, and sat—no coffee.

"Mornings only," I said. "We'll try to get done each day by one o'clock. Hopefully we'll get 'er done in two or three days at the most. How? You may well ask." I looked around the table. No one did. "Okay, I'll tell you anyway." No one laughed. *Hell, can't say as I blame 'em.*

"First, we need to get the rest of the interviews done. Kate and I will do that this morning. Bob, we don't need you for that, but if you want to sit in, you can. The more the merrier."

"Sure," Bob said. "Might as well. I've got nothing else to do."

"Good," I said. "What I'd like you to do then is sit across the room from me, where I can see you. You know the drill." He grinned. He did know it. It was a routine we used to both intimidate and look for tells.

I sat for a moment, thinking, sipping on my coffee, then said, "We now know, or at least we think we know, that our Gabrielle was not the saintly creature we assumed her to be, or at least that I assumed her to be. Now we know for sure, from what Sebastian told us, that she was playing the field. Lucy suggested Jeffery Margolis and

137

just about everyone else in pants. When we put Jeff Margolis's name to Carriere, he didn't deny it. So that one at least looks good. We'll have to see about the others. Any thoughts, Kate?"

She started to shake her head, then said, "It would be a good idea to talk to the butler again, don't you think?"

I grinned at her, and shook my head. "You really think the butler did it?"

She shrugged. "Stranger things have happened."

I had no answer for that. It would indeed be strange if the butler had done it, but in the light of what we knew now…. *Hell, she could be right.*

"Okay," I said. "We'll talk to Moore again, but first let's get the rest of the interviews completed. There's no telling what else that family has been up to, and right now, with the exception of Leo Sr., everyone we've talked to seems to have had motive and possibly opportunity.

"Tommy." I looked across the table at him. "How did your interviews go yesterday?"

He opened his iPad, flipped through several screens, and said, "These are some rare folks, Harry. The only normal one I talked to was Caspian, Leo and Vivien's son. He seems like a well-adjusted kid. The rest… well, I'll start with Georgina Walford, Evander's girlfriend. She's from New York, twenty-five, about as flighty a piece of work as I've ever come across. She's interested in only one thing: herself. They're planning to marry at Christmas."

"That's strange," I said. "Leo never mentioned it."

"No," Tommy said. "I don't think he knows. Anyway. As giddy and flighty as she is, she seems harmless enough, and she'll look good on his arm. I'd say her physical charms are probably more important to Evander than her brain. As far as I can tell, she's clean. She claims she was on the golf course with Alicia Margolis at the time of Gabby's death. Apparently they play a couple of times a week together. Georgina claims to be a very good golfer, which is how she met…. Ah, that's not important." He flipped through several more screens.

"Michael Collins, as you know, is Vivien Martan's son by her previous marriage…. I'm surprised you haven't met him. He's the general manager here. Anyway, I found him virtually unreadable. He answered my questions in monosyllables when he could and two or three word sentences when he couldn't. He was here at the resort when Gabby was killed. I haven't checked that yet, but it should be easy enough to do. As far as I could tell, though, he's clean too. Mrs. Collins…."

"Wait," I interrupted him. "Talk to me a little more about Michael Collins. Could he have been romantically involved with Gabrielle, do you think?"

He thought for a moment, shook his head. "I don't know. I didn't know about her affairs. If I had, I would have questioned him further, but I didn't, so...."

"Okay," I said. "Maybe we'll need to talk to him again, as well the butler." I cut Kate a look; she smiled back. "Go on with what you were about to say, Tommy, sorry."

"Yeah, so, Mrs. Collins, Laura, is a first-class bitch. She didn't like Gabrielle *at* all, or any of the Martans, for that matter. She thinks Gabrielle was a spoiled brat, and she's insanely jealous of her sister-in-law Alicia. The Collinses live in the suite of rooms directly below Gabrielle's—another thorn in Laura's side; she figured they should have been given the top-floor suite. Anyway, she claims that that's where she was when Gabby died. Which means she has no alibi. And that's about it."

"Do you have any suspicions about any of them?" I asked.

He thought for a moment, then said, "As I said, they're a nasty bunch, and all of them would be capable of killing, I think, but... I don't think any of the ones I interviewed did it. None of them had motives, other than Laura, and that would be a hell of a stretch."

"Okay, Tommy. So what I'd like you do today is start chasing down alibis. Start with Sebastian. Here's a list in the order I'd like it done. When we get finished with the interviews, there'll be more, and we'll help." He started to rise, but I stopped him. "Stay here until we finish up. I want you to be fully in the loop, to know what we know." He sat down again.

"Next," I said. "Tim. How about prints? Did you find anything out of the ordinary?"

He was ready for me, iPad open. "Just one thing, which I'll get to in a minute. I downloaded everything from the scanner onto my laptop: Ms. Patel's findings and the scans of the family, friends, and staff. First, Ms. Patel's people lifted latent prints on just about every surface inside all of the rooms and on the balcony. Whoever does the cleaning needs to be replaced. I ran comparisons and I found that everyone in the family, with the exception of Caspian and Georgina Walford, is represented, and I'm including Moore. The only anomaly is Jackson, the gardener. His prints were found in several places, including on the balcony rail."

"Whew," I said. "Jackson too? All of them?"

"Yup. At some time or another, they've all been in that room."

I looked at Kate. She raised her eyebrows.

"Better add Jackson to the list," I said.

141

"Um, I… uh…." Tim hesitated, looked worried.

"What?" I asked. "Spit it out."

"I…. uh. I ran all of the prints through AFIS," he said, very quickly.

"You did *what*?" I shot a quick glance at Tommy. He didn't seem bothered, but Tim's… hobbies… weren't something I needed a sworn officer to know about. "Damn it, Tim!"

"Well I had to! It's a murder case, right? I was looking for criminal matches."

"What did I tell you?" I growled. "I should fire your ass right here and now."

"Oh leave him alone," Kate said, smiling. "He was just doing his job."

I glared at her, then at Tim. He grinned back at me.

"It's okay," he said. "I got in and out without anyone knowing. I used Kate's codes and passwords—"

Kate stopped smiling very suddenly. "You did *what*?"

"Well he said we'd get you to do it, so I thought—"

"That's your problem!" Kate yelled at him. "You *think too much*."

"Oh leave him alone," I said dryly. "He was just doing his job. You said so yourself. So, did you find anything?"

"Not... really. In 2009 Georgina was charged with stealing a $3500 bracelet from a Nordstrom in New York. She copped a plea, did no time, just five years' probation. That's all. Everyone else is clean."

I looked at Tommy. He rolled his eyes and smiled.

"She was just a kid, nineteen," I said. "Otherwise she wouldn't have gotten off so lightly, which is what you won't do if you pull any more of that hacking stuff. You understand?"

"Yes, boss. Never again."

"How come I have a hard time believing you?"

He shrugged, grinned at me, then looked at Sammie, who smiled fondly at him.

Jeez.

I slid my arm out of the sling and laced my fingers together behind my neck, leaned back in my chair, and stared up at the slowly rotating fan directly above. *What the hell have I gotten myself into?*

I had no answer to that, so I leaned forward, slipped my arm back into the sling, and looked at Kate, my eyebrows raised in question. She did that thing she does with her mouth, and said nothing.

"Yeah, right?" I said, to nobody in particular. "What a friggin' mess. Look, I'm sorry. I wish I hadn't agreed to do this, but I did, and now I'm stuck with it. You guys, however, are not. I know, I know," I said, as both Kate and Bob opened their mouths to protest, "but I mean it. This is just not fair on you. I do want you to know how much I appreciate you doing it, though, all of you."

"What the hell else would we be doing for Christ's sake?" Bob asked sarcastically. "Lying around on the beach, swimming, fishing, golfing, drinking, and eating? You know how much I hate all that stuff." That brought a snicker from the rest of the group.

"Okay, let's get to it. Jacque, Wendy, Tim, Sam, you guys go enjoy yourselves. The rest of us, let's get to work. Let's get it done."

Chapter 14

We arrived at the Mount to find most of our principals sitting in the dining room waiting for us. The mood of the room was one of resentment, even hostility.

"So, you finally decided to turn up. About damn time too." Leo Jr. looked as if he might have been drinking. I looked at my watch. It was just ten minutes to ten; we were, in fact, a few minutes early.

I ignored Leo. "I could do with some coffee, if it wouldn't be too much trouble," I said to the gathering.

"In the pot on the sideboard. Help yourself." It was Vivien who spoke. I helped myself to a cup, put it down on the sideboard, opened my iPad, and then turned to face them.

"This morning we need to interview Jeffery and Alicia Margolis, you, Vivien, Evander, Mr. Collins, Mr. Jackson, and Mr. Moore, and we'll take you in that order. The rest of you may leave, but please stay close in case we need to talk to you again."

"Why me?" Michael Collins asked. "Why do you want to talk to me again? I already talked to Lieutenant Quinn."

"Yes, you did," I told him, "but we have come into some new information, and we just

145

want to run a couple of things by you. You too, Mr. Moore. So, if the rest of you will take a seat, watch TV or... something. We'll get to you all as soon as we can. Now, Mr. Margolis. If you wouldn't mind following us through to Mr. Martan's office, we'll get started.... Er... no, Mrs. Margolis," I said, as she began to get to her feet. "We need to talk to your husband alone."

"But I—"

"It's all right, Alicia. I'll manage."

I once again seated myself behind Leo Martan's desk, opened my iPad, laid it down, and set the recorder beside it. Kate sat just to my right at the end of the desk. Bob took a seat beside the window to my left, where I could see him and he could see Margolis, whom we placed in front of the desk some six feet away from it, in the center of the room, isolating him and hopefully making him very uncomfortable.

I turned on the recorder and stated the date, time, and those present for the record, and then asked Margolis if he would mind answering a few questions. He didn't.

"Kate," I said, picking up my iPad, "would you mind taking the lead?"

She picked up her own iPad, looked at Margolis, flipped through several screens, looked at him again, flipped through several more. I smiled to myself. I knew exactly what she was doing, and it worked. The longer she took, the more uncomfortable he became.

"Jeffery? Is it alright if I call you that?" she began. "Or would you like me to call you Mr. Margolis?"

"Jeff. Please call me Jeff."

She flipped through several more screens, then looked him directly in the eye, and for several seconds he held her gaze, and then he broke; he looked away.

"So, Jeffery," she said quietly. "I see from our background checks that you work for First Georgia Bank, and have since you graduated from college, correct?"

He nodded.

"Out loud, please, for the recorder."

"Yes. That's right."

"And you're quite well off: good credit, money in the bank, investments. You've done well."

"Yes, thank you."

"So, tell us about your affair with Gabrielle Martan."

The question hit him like a hammer. The color drained from his face, his knuckles whitened against the arms of the chair, and he visibly began to sweat.

"I… no…. I don't know what you're talking about. I haven't—I never…."

147

"Yes, you did," Kate said gently. "You don't think you could keep that kind of thing secret, do you? In this house? No. It seems everyone knows."

"No... no.... *No!*" He began to get to his feet.

"Sit down, please, Mr. Margolis," I said. "There's no point denying it. We know. Everyone knows."

"Oh my God, oh my God, oh my God...." He looked up at me, then at Kate. "Alicia?" he asked. "Please don't tell her. She'll.... Oh my God."

Kate shrugged. "She probably already knows," she said. "So why don't you get it off your chest. Tell us about it."

"I told you. There's—there's nothing to tell."

"Bob," Kate said. "Would you mind going to the dining room and asking Mrs. Margolis—"

"No!" Jeff shouted.

Bob smiled and stayed put.

"I'll tell you," Jeff said. "Just keep Alicia out of it, okay? All right?"

No one said anything. We just sat there and watched him sweat.

"It was just... it was.... I don't know what it was." He was wringing his hands, staring down at them. "She... I.... It was about a year ago. I

148

was on the balcony. Alicia was out, gone somewhere, I don't know. Gabby was out there too. Sunbathing. She didn't have a top on…. She caught me watching her. I couldn't help it. She was… beautiful." He looked up. "I didn't kill her. I loved her." He looked down again. We waited.

Finally: "Go on," Kate said gently.

"Well, she didn't seem to care, about me watching her, I mean. In fact, she seemed to enjoy it. I tried not to look, but… and then she started touching herself…."

Again, he stopped talking.

"Go on," Kate said.

"She had her hand inside her bikini bottom. She asked me over for a drink. I knew what would happen if I went, but I couldn't help myself. That's all. That's how it began…. I… loved her. After that… well, we saw each other often, several times a week, whenever Alicia…."

"And you're sure Alicia didn't know," I asked.

He looked up, seemingly surprised by the question. "No, she didn't know. We were careful, very careful."

I looked at Kate. She grimaced and shook her head. Fortunately, he was staring down at his hands and didn't see her. I looked at Bob. He was smiling broadly.

"Jeff," Kate said. "How can you say that? Sebastian Carriere, her fiancé, he knew. Your sister-in-law Lucy knew, which means Leo Jr. knew, and that…."

"No. Alicia didn't know. She couldn't have. If she knew, she would have said something. She would have done something. You have no idea what she's like. Her temper… she…. I would have known. I *would* have," he insisted. "I would have known."

"You say you didn't kill her. Do you have any idea who might have?"

He started to shake his head, then stopped, thought for a moment. "Sebastian. You said he knew. He did it. He killed her. If he knew, he must have been jealous. She was going to dump him. She told me. She also told me he wanted money. Hell, they all did. Leo, Evander—but she wouldn't give it to them." He paused, looked at Bob, then me, and finally Kate. "It wasn't me. I loved her. I loved her so much…." And then the tears came: just watery eyes at first, and then he was sobbing uncontrollably. We looked at each other, embarrassed, and then he seemed to snap out of it.

"I think I need to call my lawyer," he said, and again he started to get to his feet.

"There's no need for that," I said. "You're not being charged with anything. I have just one more question for you, and then you can go. Where were you between noon and two o'clock on Saturday?"

He looked down, shaking his head. "I don't have an alibi, if that's what you mean."

"Fine, but where were you?"

"I was with... I was...." He sighed. "I went for a run. I needed to be alone, to take some time to think.... I'd talked to her early that morning, from the balcony. It must have been around ten, maybe a little later. She said she wasn't going to see me anymore. We argued. She wouldn't listen. I didn't know what to do.... I walked for miles. I walked the golf course, to the ninth green, and from there to the beach, and then I followed the shore until.... I don't know. When I came back, the police were here. You were here. I couldn't believe she was... that she was... dead."

"Why don't you go clean yourself up before someone sees you?" I said. "But stay close. We may need to talk to you again."

He stood slowly, nodded twice, and then turned and walked to the door, his shoulders slumped forward, like an old man. I kinda felt sorry for him.

"Okay," I said, when the door had closed behind him. "Unless he's one hell of an actor, I'm inclined to believe him: I don't think he did it. What do you think?"

"I think he's a hell of an actor," Bob said. "What the hell else is he going to say but 'I didn't kill her'? She told him she was going to dump him. He went around to talk to her, lost his temper, and smacked her over the head. He thinks he's killed her. He tosses her off the balcony to make it look like she killed herself. No, we can't rule him out; not yet."

"Kate?" I asked.

"Come on, Harry. I can't believe you're taking him at his word. You know better. We've seen them all. They're all believable until they get caught. He's no different. How many times have you told me that we're not in the business of taking anyone's word for anything? I'm not going to say he did it, but I don't think we can rule him out."

I nodded, slowly, thinking. She was right, but that old instinct of mine had kicked in, and I was fairly sure he was telling the truth.

"Okay. We'll set judgment on him aside, for now. Let's get his good wife in here and see what she has to say."

Chapter 15

Tommy was right. This was indeed an unusual family, about as dysfunctional a bunch as I'd ever run across. The kids were spoiled beyond recovery and the in-laws were a bunch of predatory gold diggers, but Alicia Margolis broke the mold.

Like the other women in the family, she was good looking. At thirty-five, she was five years older than her husband. I say she was good looking, but her age and long hours in the sun were beginning to take their toll. Dressed in white shorts, a white blouse, and white tennis shoes, she was about five foot eight, slim, busty, with a heart-shaped face, a nose that was slightly too large, and a pair of wide blue eyes, all surrounded by a halo of dark red hair, the color of which could only have come out of a bottle, and probably cost the Earth.

"Sit down, Mrs. Margolis," I said. "Thank you for agreeing to talk to us."

"As if I had any damn choice," she snapped. Her voice was low, and in any other circumstance would have been her most attractive quality. Here, however, it was tinged with overtones that bordered on contempt. "And what have you been saying to my husband? He charged into the dining room as if the devil were after

153

him. White as damned sheet. Frightened to death. Have you been accusing him of something?"

I leaned back in my chair and looked at Bob. He nodded and turned to look at her.

"We're not accusing him of anything, exactly," I said. "We were just questioning him about his affair with Gabrielle."

If I was expecting a response, it wasn't the one I got.

She snorted. "Is that all?"

I waited for her to continue, but she didn't. She folded her arms and stared across the desk at me.

"You knew about it?" I asked, unable to keep the surprise out of my voice.

"Of course I did. D'you think I'm blind? I know Jeffery does. Silly little man."

"And you didn't confront him?" Kate asked.

"Why would I? If I had, he probably would have stopped. As it was, while he was screwing her, at least he wasn't bothering me. And anyway, I really didn't see any harm in it."

"By that," I said dryly, "I have to assume that you had something of your own going?"

"Assume all you want."

I looked at Bob. He gave a slight shake of his head. He seemed as dumbfounded as I was. I decided to take the direct approach.

"Mrs. Margolis. Are you having an illicit sexual affair?"

At that, she burst out laughing. She shook her head, smiled sideways at me. It wasn't a pretty sight.

"Am I screwing someone other than my husband, do you mean? Yes."

"And who would that be?"

"None of your damned business," she snapped.

"One of the family?" I watched her closely. And there it was: her eyes flicked away from mine for just a split second; the slight pause before she replied was barely perceptible, but it too was there.

"Don't be ridiculous," she snapped. But it was too late. Bob had caught it too.

"So who is it?" I asked, again watching her closely. "Michael, Leo Jr., Evander... no? How about Caspian... Moore... Jackson?" She smiled and said nothing. And then I had an epiphany. I remembered what Tommy had said earlier, about her being out on the golf course.

"How about...." I paused, smiled. "How about... Georgina?"

The smile left her face, but in an instant it was back. There was no humor in it. I had her, and she knew it.

"So," I continued. "You're gay, gay or bi. And you're having a fling with Georgina. Does your husband know you're a switch hitter?"

"Hah," she said. "You have it all wrong. I'm not gay and I don't have flings."

"So it's serious then, your affair with Georgina?"

She didn't answer. I knew right then that she wasn't going to say another word on the subject, so I changed it.

"Where were you between noon and two o'clock on Saturday?" I already knew, but I asked anyway.

She sighed, looked down at her hands clasped together in her lap, then looked up and said, defiantly, "I was with Georgina, on the golf course. You can check with her."

"Did you kill Gabrielle?"

She looked me right in the eye. "No, I did not."

"Do you know who did?"

"No, I do not!"

Was that a hesitation?

"How about your mother, Mrs. Martan?"

"Are you out of your mind? Of course not!"

I smiled at her and said, "That will be all, Mrs. Margolis. You can leave now but, as they say in the movies, don't leave town."

156

Well, I thought it was funny, even if she didn't. Whatever. The room shook as she slammed the door on her way out.

"Damn," Bob said. "Who would have thought it?"

I shook my head. I was surprised, but I shouldn't have been. I've run across stranger things in my time, that's for sure.

"Weirder and weirder," Kate said. "I'm not sure I can keep track of the mess, of who's diddling who. Whew."

"Right, but did she do it?"

"Hell. She could have," Bob said. "Maybe she was pissed that her husband was screwing her stepsister. That would be motive, and she has no alibi. Georgina could have helped her throw the girl over the balcony."

I looked at my watch. It was almost a quarter to eleven. I thought about Amanda. *She's probably out by the pool. I wish to hell I was.*

I sighed. "Let's get Vivien in here. The sooner we finish these interviews, the sooner we can enjoy the afternoon."

I flipped the lock screen on my phone and called Vivien.

Chapter 16

"This is quite a family you have here, Mrs. Martan," I said as she took her seat in front of the desk. Once again, I was hoping to throw her off balance, but I was disappointed. A lady she was, in every sense of the word. Cool, haughty, even a little disdainful. She sat rigidly erect, chin up, her back not touching the chair, her legs crossed at the ankles, and her hands folded together in her lap.

She was only forty-nine years old, and she looked barely thirty. Her blonde hair was styled short, much like Amanda's. Her sleeveless black sheath dress must have cost a couple of grand, probably more. Whatever. It fit her perfectly.

"I'm sure I have no idea what you mean," she said. "I'm proud of them all, as is their father."

"I'm sure you are," I said dryly. "Your daughter's fooling around with your stepson's girlfriend. Your son-in-law was having an affair with the victim, his sister-in-law. Leo Jr. is one step from federal prison, and God only knows what the rest of them are up to. Yes, you have a lot to be proud of, Mrs. Martan."

"Think what you will," she replied. "They, all of them, are victims of their father's lax outlook on parenting. He's given them everything they ever wanted; not just his own children, mine too. Yes, they're spoiled—"

158

"Spoiled!" Kate was incredulous. "Spoiled? This is the single most dysfunctional family I've had the dubious pleasure of encountering in my entire career. Spoiled, you say? One of them is a *killer*!"

Finally, a reaction. The color went out of Vivien's face. Her eyes were ablaze with anger, but she took a deep breath and held it together. Her hands, though, were clasped tightly together; the knuckles were white.

"Mr. Starke. I'm a busy woman. I have better thing to do than sit here while you and your colleagues insult me and my family. Would you please get on with this... this... *farce*, so that I can go about the rest of my day?"

I nodded. "Alright. Did you know what was going on?" I already knew the answer, but I thought it was worth getting her denial on record. Her answer, though, was a surprise.

"I knew that Jeffery was having an affair with Gabrielle, yes. I also know about Leo's woes, but they will be resolved quite shortly. You don't think for one minute that his father will let him go to prison, do you?" She paused for a moment, looked down, and seemed to be contemplating her fingers, which were now drumming against her thighs.

She gave me a strange look, her head tilted to one side, the corners of her mouth turned down. I thought for a moment she was about to cry, but she didn't.

"And yes," she said, resignation in her voice, "I've known about Alicia's sexual preferences for a long time, since she was fourteen, in fact. She married Jeffery purely out of convention. She doesn't love him. There will be no children. Georgina isn't her first love, nor will she be her last, I'm sure."

The room was quiet. Inwardly, I was shaking my head. *This poor woman is devastated. My God. How the hell does she cope with it all? Whoa.* I had a sudden thought.

"Was she... was Alicia in love with Gabrielle?" I asked in a low voice.

The question didn't faze her one bit. "No."

"How do you know?"

"I know my daughter. Gabrielle wasn't her type. Gabrielle was a lazy, good-for-nothing slut, and didn't care who knew it. Alicia's preferences are exactly the opposite. Georgina is smart, discreet, attractive, and an athlete, as have been all of Alicia's... friends."

I looked hard at her. "Did she kill Gabrielle?"

That brought a smile to her face. "What am I supposed to say to that? Of course she didn't. And even if I thought she did, I wouldn't tell you, now would I?"

I wasn't sure, but I thought it was a little forced. I looked at Bob. Evidently he wasn't convinced either, because the only reaction I got from him was a slight shrug.

"Did you kill her?" Kate asked.

"No!"

I was watching her face for… anything that might indicate she was lying. I saw nothing. I glanced at Bob. He grimaced and shook his head, once.

"You must have thought about it. Do you have any idea who might have?" I asked.

She shook her head. "No! Now. If that's all…."

"Just one more question, for the record, if you don't mind, Mrs. Martan."

She stood facing me, a proud and beautiful woman by any standard.

"Where were you between noon and two o'clock on Saturday?"

"With my husband. We had lunch together at noon. We went for a short walk. Arrived back at the house just after one, and then retired for our afternoon nap. That usually only lasts for thirty minutes or so. My husband is a very busy man, as you well know. On Saturday we had been in our rooms for only ten minutes or so when Moore called him. Now, if you don't mind, I'd like to leave."

"Thank you ma'am," I said, and without another word she glided out of the room as if she were on a runway. Impressive, but also kind of pathetic. I almost felt sorry for her.

"Well, that was interesting," Kate said. "I guess we can finally cross someone off the list."

I nodded. "Yup. Who's next? No, wait. I need a bathroom break and some coffee. Let's go find some."

Chapter 17

It seems coffee was something of a twenty-four-hour service at the Mount. The double BUNN brewer on the sideboard in the dining room had a full pot of decaf and another of regular, along with two plates of pastries. I went for the regular coffee and a cherry Danish, and so did Bob, but he took two pastries; Kate poured herself a cup of decaf—no food—and we took ourselves out onto the patio, where we were once again treated to the stunning views of the north side of Calypso Key.

The golf course meandered all the way around the great house, then made a right and headed for the low line of hills that formed a backdrop for the great green ribbons and buttons that were the fairways and greens. It was a balmy day. The sky an unbroken field of azure. The palms that lined the fairways fluttered in the breeze, and there was not a soul on the course. *I wish to hell I was out there. Maybe another day.*

We took seats around a small table, under a lime green sun umbrella, and for a quiet moment or two we did little more than stare out at the view, each coddling thoughts of our own. Me? My head was in a whirl. Already ideas were beginning to form, but until we'd finished the interviews I would have to let them cook. One thing I knew for sure: we were dealing with the family from hell.

"Okay," I said, finally breaking the silence. "We've only got a few minutes. I don't want to be here all day. Do either of you have any thoughts about what we've seen and heard so far?"

"I'm thinking that without any physical evidence, we're going to have a tough time pinning it on anyone at all," Kate said. I had to agree with her.

"Bob?" I asked.

He thought for a moment. "I like Leo Jr. for it. He has a hell of a motive. Either he gets his hands on some big money fast, or he's in big trouble."

"He's in big trouble regardless," Kate said. "But his dad will bail him out, cover the losses. Vivien is right. He won't let his eldest son go to jail."

"I agree," I said, "but they all, with the exception of the Margolises and the staff, are in dire need of a robust injection of cash, even Carriere, the fiancé, and I don't think we've seen it all yet."

"Uh-huh," Kate said, "but if we're considering motives: the Margolises might not need money, but they have plenty more going for them: jealousy and security for Alicia. If she thought Gabrielle was planning to dump

Sebastian and take Jeffy-baby away from her, that would be motive enough, even if she is having an affair. These people don't give up their riches and positions easily. As for Jeffery: if Gabby was about to dump him, a loss of temper would have been all it took for him to pick up the nearest heavy object and whack her over the head with it."

"I'm still liking Leo Jr. for it," Bob said. "He's a rabid son of a bitch, and then there's his wife, Lucy. What a piece of work she is, and everything you said, Kate, about the Margolises, works for that family too."

"Well," I said, "According to Tom Quinn, we can rule out Caspian, and we've ruled out the mother… but the daughter, as you said, is iffy at best. Alicia. Hmmm. She has an alibi, but it's tenuous to say the least, and the same can be said for Georgina; they alibi each other. And she's a big strong girl, Georgina is. She could have helped Alicia tip Gabby off the balcony. Nope. We don't have enough yet. We need to talk to the rest of the family. Evander, I have a feeling, will be just the same as the rest: dysfunctional to the bone. And the Collinses… more of the same, I shouldn't wonder. Let's get back. As I said, I want to get back to Amanda."

Bob, with a big cheesy grin on his face, said, "And I—"

"Don't even go there," Kate said, but she was smiling all the same.

Chapter 18

Evander Martan sauntered into the office with a wide grin on his face and his hands in his pockets. He looked a lot like his older brother: same height, same brown hair, same blue eyes—and same receding hairline, despite being only twenty-eight.

He was slimmer than Leo Jr., though, and I immediately got the idea, from the indolent way he carried himself, that he let very little worry him, let alone get him down. He was dressed in swim trunks at least two sizes too big and a T-shirt that proclaimed *One tequila, two tequila, three tequila, floor.* By the look of him I figured the saying was less a joke than the truth.

"Hey y'all," he said, in an affected Southern accent that left a lot to be desired. "What's happenin'?"

"Sit down, Mr. Martan," I said, waving a hand at the chair in front of the desk.

"Hey. Call me Evan, okay? Everybody does."

"Fine. Evan, then." He sat—no, he *sprawled.* Legs out, arms folded, head cocked to one side, that silly smile still plastered across his face.

"So," he said. "Who the hell done it? Do you know yet?"

166

"We were hoping you might be able to tell us," I said.

What the hell does Georgina see in this clown, I wonder? No wonder she's sleeping with Alicia.

"Where were you from noon until two on Saturday?" Kate asked him.

He looked at her. His eyes widened slightly, and he sucked his bottom lip into his mouth. I knew exactly what he was thinking. *Don't go there. You'll regret it.*

"Whoa," he said, allowing his lip to flip back into place. "What are you doin' after work?"

"Maybe I'll be locking your ass away," Kate said testily.

"My, my. Touchy, ain't we. Just foolin' with ya. Where was I?" He stared up at the ceiling, seemingly deep in thought. "Dunno!"

"What do you mean, you don't know?" Kate asked.

He shrugged. "I mean I *don't... know.*"

"You don't know where you were when your sister was murdered?" I asked. "Pull the other one, sonny. Answer the damned question or I'll have Tommy Quinn come and haul your ass off to Charlotte Amalie."

He straightened up a little, staring at me through slitted eyes. "That's a bit optimistic, my friend," he said. The fake southern accent was gone. "I was here. In my study, writing. I'm

167

writing a book, a novel, a crime thriller about a crooked cop and—"

"Then why didn't you say that in the first place?" Kate interrupted.

He shrugged. "How long is this bullshit going to take? I have things to do."

"Did you kill your sister?" I asked.

"Why in God's name would I do that? Of course I didn't."

"Money. You need money. She dies, you get to split her inheritance with your brother."

"I don't need her money," he said derisively. "Don't you know who we are, man?"

"Oh, I know who you are all right, and I know you need money in the worst way."

He straightened a little more in his chair. I flipped through several screens on my iPad, found the one I was looking for, and began to read aloud.

"Evander Louis Martan. Twenty-eight. Educated at Henry and Adam High School. Attended Charleston Technical College but dropped out after six months. Employment: none, ever. Finances: inherited sixteen million from your mother on your twenty-fifth birthday. Liquid assets...."

"Okay, okay," he interrupted, "so I like to enjoy life. So what?"

"So you have no assets," I said flatly. "No investments. And when this report was drawn up, you had precisely $1,832 in the bank. What the hell did you do with the sixteen million?"

"That, my friend, is none of your damn business. Now get on with this crap or I'm outa here."

"You're right. It normally *would* be none of my business, but the several facts that your sister was murdered, that you're just about flat broke, and that because of her death you'll inherit nearly fifteen million dollars *makes* it my business. All of that also means that you had motive enough to kill her, and I think you did kill her. Your fingerprints are all over her room." *A bit of an exaggeration, but what the hell.*

"I think you hit her over the head," I continued, "knocked her out, and then threw her off the balcony, and I think you did it for the money."

I was stunned when he burst out laughing.

"What the hell is so funny?" I asked.

He looked first at Kate, then at Bob. "Okay, I'll bite," he said. "Which one of you? Bad cop good cop, right? I know who the hell the bad cop is, so who's the good cop…. It's you, isn't it, gorgeous," he said to Kate. "Do you have a uniform? I love women in uniforms, and I bet you—"

169

"That's enough, damn it," Bob growled, rising quickly to his feet. "Another word and I'll bust your damned nose." He made a grab for him, but he wasn't quick enough. Evander spun sideways out of his chair, laughing, avoiding Bob's grasp by no more than a hair.

"Whoa, *two* bad cops. That's *too* funny."

I watched in amazement as he headed for the door, leaving Bob hovering over the now-empty chair.

"You stupid rubes," he said. "If I wanted to kill her I could have done it a thousand times, and if I had, I'd have hidden her so she'd never have been found."

"But then," I said quietly, "you would have had to wait seven years before you could get your hands on the cash, and you couldn't do that, now could you? No, Evan. You killed her, and we'll get you. Count on it."

He didn't answer. He simply grinned at me as he opened the door.

"Stay close by, Evan." I said, but he'd already closed the door behind him.

I looked at Kate, then at Bob. Both were smiling.

"No, Evan," Kate mimicked me—badly, I might add; her voice was practically a falsetto. "You killed her, and we'll get you. Count on it." I could tell she was holding back laughter. "What the hell was that about, Harry?"

170

I couldn't help myself; I smiled too. "Just giving him a little something to worry about, is all. He's a bright boy, though. A whole lot brighter than he would have us believe."

"Oh we got that," she said. "But I'm almost positive he didn't kill her. Bob?"

"I don't think so. His brother Leo, yes, but him…. Nah. What do you think, Harry?"

"I think we'd better keep an open mind. He has a motive and no alibi that he's willing to share, so that means opportunity. His prints were found in her room, but so were those of almost all of the others, so without some physical evidence to put him there at the time of her death…. Well, you two know as well as I do that we have nothing on any of them, including surfer dude Evander."

I looked at my watch. It was only 11:35. Somehow, it seemed much later. I always thought time flew when you were having fun, and we were having fun, right?

"You know," I said, more to myself than to Kate and Bob, "he could have done it. He…."

I was thinking about the smart-assed, sideways look he'd given me when he called us stupid rubes. That was twice someone in this family from hell had called us that, but the way Evander had said it…. Well, I was certain he meant it. He figured he was a whole lot smarter than we were. That being so, I also did a little

171

figuring: *He thinks he knows something we don't know. What could that be, I wonder?*

"Harry?" Kate asked. "Are you still with us?"

I shook my head, coming back down to earth. "Yeah, but I was thinking that maybe this guy is not only smarter than he would have us believe, but that he either did kill Gabrielle, or knows who did."

I looked at my watch again. 11:38. I sighed. "Let's get on with it. Who's next on the agenda?"

It was Michael Collins, Vivien's son. Either him or his wife, Laura.

Chapter 19

"Let's try something different," I said, pulling a second chair up beside the one already in front of the desk. "Let's do them both together, play one off the other. What do you think?"

"I'll give them a call," Bob said, pulling his phone out.

Just a few minutes later, the couple was seated together in front of the desk.

Tommy Quinn was right about one thing: Michael Collins was all but unreadable, and he had his game face on. Laura Collins, not so much. In fact, she looked angry.

As the general manager of the Windward Resort Michael was dressed as such, in a dark gray business suit, white shirt, and blue tie. He was of medium build, maybe five foot eleven, slim, tanned, and quite unremarkable. Laura, however, looked like a younger version of her mother-in-law. She wore her platinum blonde hair cut short at the back and long at the sides, so that it covered her ears and created a frame for her not unlovely face: the nose was a little on the small side, and her eyes had a slightly oriental slant to them—or was that just her makeup? Her clothes were noticeably expensive: a short, flared lace skirt with a slim gold chain around her waist, a sleeveless white top, and gold-trimmed, black leather sandals.

173

I'd watched them both come in, and I had no doubt which was the dominant personality. He walked a step behind her. He waited until she chose a chair, and only when she had seated herself did he sit down himself, and when he did, he looked more like a librarian than a hotel manager. His shoulders were slightly slumped, and I watched him take out a pair of gold-rimmed glasses and put them on; they completed the picture. He was there only because he was married to her, and she was married to him only because of who he was, I was sure of it, and nobody had even said a word.

"Thank you," I said, "for giving up your time."

He said nothing. She nodded, and made a show of crossing her legs—and when I say show, I mean just that. Sharon Stone had nothing on this lady, and this lady had nothing on under her skirt. And she knew that I knew, and she didn't care. The angry look on her face melted away, and she smiled demurely at me.

Hell. It's a good thing Amanda's not here.

I looked sideways at Kate, and I could tell by the expression on her face that she'd seen it too. I glanced across the room at Bob.

Nope, he's missed out…. I mean he missed it… no, from where he is he can't see up her— Jeez, Harry!

174

I dragged my mind out of the gutter, looked at her, and….

Oh, that smile is talking to me.

"Mr. Collins," I said. "Where were you between noon and two o'clock yesterday? Do you remember?"

"I was at the resort all day, working."

"And I would have no trouble confirming that?" I asked.

"No. I was on duty most of the day except for…."

"Lunch?" I asked with a smile. "And what time was lunch?"

"From noon until one."

"And did anyone see you while you were at lunch?"

"I'm sure they did, but I can't tell you who. I like a little time to myself. So I eat outside, on the patio. I'm sure someone did see me… well the waiters saw me, certainly. John, yes, John, and Ruby. They waited on me."

"How about you, Mrs. Collins? Where were you?"

"I was in our suite on the second floor, alone. I don't have an alibi. That is what you call it, isn't it?" She was smiling, but there was little humor in it.

I nodded, and turned my attention again to Michael Collins.

"Were you having an affair with Gabrielle Martan, Mr. Collins?"

"Excuse me?"

"It's quite simple, Michael," Laura said, uncrossing and recrossing her legs, gifting both me and Kate with a glimpse of... well, you get the idea. "They want to know if you were screwing our dear stepsister. You along with everyone else in this godforsaken family."

He looked stricken, the first real emotion I'd seen on his face since he came into the room, and yep, Tommy was right. She was a first-class bitch all right, and now I had no doubt about something else he'd said. Laura Collins had not liked Gabrielle, and that, I thought, was putting it mildly.

"I gather, Mrs. Collins, that you didn't like Gabrielle."

"Like her? No. I didn't like her. She was a spoiled little rich kid and she made it very plain that she didn't like her stepbrother and me. Nor did she like the Margolises. In fact, she hated Alicia."

"But she was having an affair with Jeffery Margolis...?"

"I didn't say she didn't like his dick," she all but snarled. "He is, so she told us whenever she got the chance, exceptionally well endowed. And his wasn't the only one she liked. Have you talked to the butler?" Before I could answer, she continued, "Butler my derriere. The man is Leo's bodyguard. He was a Navy Seal, or some such animal."

I flipped through Tim's report on my iPad. She was right. Moore had been a Seal, honorably discharged, but there were no other details of interest.

"No," she continued as I flipped through the report, "Michael was not—I repeat, not—having an affair with Gabrielle. Look at him. He doesn't have it in him, do you my dear?"

Jeez. This really is a live one.

I looked at Michael, and I immediately felt sorry for him. He was obviously well and truly under his wife's thumb, but....

"Can you account for your fingerprints being in her room?" I asked, knowing damn well that she could.

"Of course. Gabby was always throwing parties. We were there with the rest of the family on several occasions. I'm sure you must have found theirs too. I couldn't be specific, but they, and we, were almost all there at one time or another, and they will confirm it. So there you are. Make of it what you will."

"You hated her didn't you," Kate said. It was the first time she'd spoken. "Why?"

"I'm not really sure, other than because she was totally spoiled and resented her stepmother, Michael's mother, and the rest of us interlopers, as she called us to our faces whenever she lost her temper, which was quite often, by the way. She… she just wasn't likeable."

"Did you kill her?" I asked, watching her carefully.

"No. I did not kill her. She wasn't that important. Again, I suggest you talk to the butler. May we leave now?" she asked sweetly.

"One more minute, if you please, Mrs. Collins. You keep suggesting Victor Moore might be involved. What exactly do you know?"

She took a deep breath, closed her eyes, cocked her head to one side, and let the breath out slowly through her lips, making a spluttering sound.

"Victor Moore is a pig. He once tried to rape me. Fortunately, Sebastian heard me calling for help and saved me."

"So that's why you think he might have killed her?"

She shrugged. "It's possible. You probably know that better than I do. I do know that he was screwing her. She told me so herself. Now, if that's all, I need to go to the stables and Michael needs to go back to work, don't you dear?"

The poor man didn't reply. Instead he rose to his feet, walked to the door, opened it, and walked out without a backward look, leaving his lovely wife still seated in front of us.

"Well," she said, "I wonder what's gotten into him." And then she uncrossed her legs—*Jeez*—rose to her feet, and followed her husband out of the room, closing the door behind her.

For more than a minute, the room sat in a silence that was palpable enough to cut with a knife.

It was Kate who eventually did the cutting. "In all my years, I have never met one quite like that."

"Quite like what?" Bob asked.

I looked at him and shook my head.

"I saw that, Harry," she said. "I hope you can live with yourself, especially when you meet with Amanda this afternoon."

"What?" Bob and I said it together.

"You know what," she said. "I thought your eyeballs were going to pop right out of your head. I thought you'd put all that stuff behind you."

"What?" Bob said again.

"What the hell was I supposed to do, Kate? It was right in front of my damned face. I didn't see you looking away either." For a minute, I thought she was going to slap me. Instead she said, "It was quite a show, though, wasn't it?

"*What?*" Bob all but yelled.

"Nothing you need worry your ugly head about, my love," Kate said to him, at the same time gifting me with a grin. "And be sure you tell Amanda. If you don't…."

"Shut up," I said, smiling at her.

"Okay. Now. After that little show… I mean *encounter*, I want to talk to Moore again. Let's get him in here."

Chapter 20

Two minutes after Kate called Moore to ask him to come by, there was a knock on the office door. "Good afternoon, Mr. Moore," I said, offering him my hand. "Please, sit down."

He shook my hand, sat, then turned slightly in his seat and looked at Bob. Bob's face was a mask, expressionless.

"Okay," he said. "I'm here. Why? I've already talked to you."

"We want to know exactly what your relationship with Gabrielle was. We've been told by no less than three members of the family and... well, never mind, that you were indeed having an affair with her."

"I told you," he growled, "that I wasn't."

"What about Laura Collins?"

He frowned. "What about her?"

"She said you tried to rape her."

"I *what*?"

"She said," Kate said after a moment, her voice low and threatening, "that you assaulted her. That Sebastian Carriere stopped you. It's easy enough to check. We can simply ask Sebastian."

"It's not true. She came onto me one night during the summer last year. It was on the patio,

181

late. She was drunk. She grabbed hold of me and I pushed her away. She tried again. She went wild, attacking me, screaming. And yes, Mr. Carriere, he pulled her off me. Ask him. He'll tell you."

"Oh, we will. You can count on it."

"Why would these people say you were having an affair with Gabrielle if it wasn't true?" I asked.

"God. Do I really have to answer that for you? You've met them all. They, every one of them, are the product of—what's the word they use these days… affluenza, right? Too much money, too little control, and even less early-life guidance. They're a mess. All of them. Why do they think I was having an affair with Gabrielle? Because they're a bunch of twisted… yes, I was very close to Gabrielle, and everyone knew it, but… I can only think that it was misconstrued."

Yes. I could see where he was coming from. But there was something about the way he kept avoiding my eye. Inwardly, I was shaking my head, but other than jealous family gossip, there was nothing to prove any of it.

I flipped through the screens on my iPad, located the information Tim had provided, and said, "You were in the Navy for seven years. A Seal, so I understand. A butler is a strange occupation for—"

"You know damn well I'm more than a butler," he interrupted. "I provide Mr. Martan

182

with security. He trusts me. Where he goes, I go. He's known me since I was teenager, since before I joined the Navywho the murder was. He knew what I was and when I got out he asked me to work for him, simple as that. He's paranoid about being kidnapped."

"Okay, Mr. Moore. Just one more thing. Maybe you can answer it, maybe not. CSI found Jackson's fingerprints in Gabrielle's rooms. What reason would the gardener have for visiting her, do you know? Was he...?"

He smiled, shook his head, and said, "No. He wasn't. He's the gardener. He visits almost every room in the house every day. He provides fresh flowers."

And there it was. Simple enough, and entirely believable.

"All right, Mr. Moore. That's all for now. Thanks for your time."

"I...." He hesitated, shook his head. "Never mind. It's not important."

"Okay," Kate said, as the door closed behind him. "I think he *was* having an affair with her, and that—"

"Don't."

"Don't what?"

"You know what," I said.

She smiled. "But I do," she said quietly.

"Bob?" I asked.

"He's as good a choice as any, I suppose. I don't think we're gonna get it done, Harry. Not without some physical evidence. He's right. This is the weirdest bunch of cats I've ever run into. It could have been any one of them."

Kate got to her feet. "That's all of them except for Jackson, the gardener," she said. "Want me to go get him?"

"No, I don't think so. We know why he was in her rooms. I think we've already talked to the killer. Nobody's said a bad word about Jackson. We'll leave him out, for now. We can always talk to him later, if we think there's any need for it. For now, I need to talk to Leo Sr., bring him up to speed. I'd like you both to remain here while I talk to him."

I made the call and asked him to join us, and less than five minutes later he was seated in front of me and Kate; Bob remained seated by the window.

"So?" he asked, somewhat impatiently. "What have you discovered?"

I leaned back in his desk chair and looked at him closely.

How much of this mess do you already know? I thought. *More to the point, how much more do you really* want *to know?*

I took a deep breath. "With the exception of Jackson, we've completed the initial round of interviews." He leaned forward, his elbows on his knees, hands clasped together in front of him.

"And?" he asked.

"One thing I know for sure is that we've already talked to Gabrielle's killer."

"Do you have any idea who it is?"

"No, but I'm narrowing it down.... Tell me about Victor Moore."

"He's my butler. I've known him for years. Why do you ask? Surely you don't suspect him of—"

"He's not exactly Jeeves, is he? Where did you find him?"

"I didn't find him. I knew his parents, grew up with them. No. He's not exactly the archetypal butler, but he looks after my special needs very well."

"Did you know he was having an affair with your daughter?" I asked, trying for a little shock treatment. It had the opposite effect.

"No he wasn't." He smiled. "That's just family gossip. Oh, he was close to her. She was only seven when he joined me eighteen years ago. She took to him immediately; loved him like a brother. He always had time for her silliness, and she appreciated it. When she needed anything—advice, someone to talk to, a shoulder to cry on—it was him she would go to, not me. And yes, I do think he loved her, but not in that way."

I glanced at Bob. He nodded. He believed him, and so did I.

"Well," I said, "I think we're done here for the day. Can you get someone to take us back to the resort, please?"

"I'll do it myself. Would you like to go right now? I'll have Moore bring the car around to the front and I'll meet you there in... five minutes."

"So," I said to Kate, as we gathered up our bits and pieces, "still think the butler did it?"

"Right now, yeah, I'd say he's as good a choice as any. You?"

"I still like Alicia, Jeff, Leo Jr., and Sebastian... in that order."

"Bob?"

"Leo and Jeff and maybe Alicia. What was all that stuff about Laura, about a show?"

"You'll have to get Harry to tell you all about it," Kate said sarcastically. "He thoroughly enjoyed himself."

I grinned at her. Hell, it was true. Married I might have been, but I'm still a man, for God's sake.

Chapter 21

Monday November 14, Evening

Dinner that evening was something special. The menu included conch salad, cracked conch, and blue crab claws for appetizers, and huge grilled spiny lobster tails imported from Mayaguana for the main course, served with crispy coconut grouper steaks and red beans and rice. For dessert, a choice of either pineapple or chocolate bread pudding—or both, if you were Amanda. All of this was followed by unlimited cups of Jamaican Blue Mountain Coffee; the real thing, not the blend. It wasn't until later that I learned Amanda had brought the beans with her; she'd plundered my special reserves, bless her. Coffee was followed by large snifters of Remy Martin XO.

It was inevitable, then, that the conversation turned to the investigation. My father, being the lawyer he is, wanted a complete breakdown. Me, being the tired and ill-used PI I figured I was, refused to go that route. I made him settle for the short version.

"Tell them about the floor show, Harry."

"Laura Collins, you mean? Hell, Kate. You were there. You saw it all, same as I did. You tell them."

"But you had the best seat in the house, didn't you, Harry?"

"Do tell, *Harry*," Amanda said sweetly.

"Oh hell, the woman wasn't wearing underwear. That's all. It was no big deal."

"So that's what it was," Bob said. "Damn. I did miss the show, didn't I?"

"So you did, my love," Kate said. "But if you're a good bear… who knows what rewards you might receive later."

His face was a picture. I had never seen him so embarrassed. But his red face belied his feelings.

I think he truly loves her. Wow.

"So." My father was not about to give it up. "What's next?"

"What's next," I said dryly, "is nothing, at least not for the next day or two. I need some input from forensics and the ME in St. Thomas. Until I get that, I've done all I can. I'll spend some time with Amanda: I want to take her back to the *Rhone*, this time with scuba gear. I'll also let you cheat me at golf. Bob, you wanna go eighteen holes with my dad and me?"

He said he did, but I wasn't sure he was too enthusiastic about it. Still, he played a wicked ten handicap and would give my old man a run for his money.

And so the third day of my new life slowly wound down. I was thrilled with the idea that the next several days would belong to me and whomever I wanted to include, and no one else.

Chapter 22

"No work today my love," I said as I placed a cup of coffee on the nightstand beside her. "I'm all yours. Better yet," I said, climbing back into bed beside her, "you're all mine. C'mere." I made a grab for her, but she wriggled away.

"Harry. No. I need the bathroom and my coffee." Like a greased snake, she slipped out of my grasp and ran to the bathroom. She was gone for maybe five minutes, and when she returned she'd done her hair and looked fabulous. She kneeled on the bed, leaned in, and brushed my lips with hers—she tasted minty. It took my breath away. I put my arms around her, but she pushed back.

"Patience, big boy. I haven't had my coffee yet."

And boy did she ever take her time. I watched as she sat on the edge of the bed, her cup cradled in both hands, her eyes closed as she sipped. It was quite an act, and I was mesmerized.

Finally she set the cup down, turned her head, and looked at me over her shoulder, chin down, eyes half closed, and gifted me with a smile that, if I hadn't known better, I would have taken for pure evil.

"Ready?" she asked in a low voice.

189

I grinned, nodded, put my hands behind my neck, and lay back on the pillow.

She climbed over me, straddled me, sat on my belly, took the hem of her white satin chemise in both hands and, in one smooth move, stripped it off over her head, stretching upward like some great cat as she did so. It was the sexiest move I'd ever seen, designed to do nothing other than blow my mind... and it did.

The next hour passed in a dream, a swirling cloud of utter bliss. To this day, I remember every touch, every whisper, every kiss. And all before eight o'clock in the morning.

We hit the shower, had some breakfast, and headed out to the beach. I insisted we leave our phones at the cottage. I felt naked without mine, but I was determined to have some time alone with her.

"Harry," Amanda said later, as we lay stretched out side by side. "I've been thinking about what you said, about the spot of blood on the carpet. That it wasn't spatter; that it fell from Gabrielle's head when she was moved. Suppose it wasn't hers? What if it belonged to the killer? It could. Couldn't it?"

I looked at her, smiled at her.

"What?" she asked.

"I already thought of that. I really have to try not to leave you alone anymore." I was joking.

"You've been watching too much TV, too much CSI."

"Pig!" She punched my arm. I screwed up my face in mock pain.

"Oh my God, Harry, I'm so sorry." She was mortified. "I forgot about your arm."

I jumped up, grabbed her hand, pulled her to her feet, slung her over my shoulder like a sack of flour, and ran with her, squealing, into the ocean. For ten minutes we played together like a couple of kids, running and splashing, tackling each other until finally, exhausted, we staggered back up the beach and flopped down on the towels. And we lay there, holding hands, breathing hard, staring up at the scudding white clouds; it was a beautiful moment.

"You know," I said after some minutes, "what you said, about the blood. I don't see how it could belong to the killer, but it's a good thought. Sheesh, I might be able to make a detective of you yet.... But we couldn't get that lucky... could we?"

"Come on, Harry. You don't need to get lucky. You're the king of deception and trickery. Oh, don't look at me like that. You know what I mean. Tell them what you found, and that you think the blood belongs to the killer and that you want everyone to provide a DNA sample. If it does belong to the killer, it could cause him to panic. If not, you've lost nothing. You'll just need to watch them all carefully…. Stop laughing at me, you ass!"

"I wasn't laughing at you! Well I was, but not the way you're thinking. I was laughing at how well you've gotten to know me, and how far we've come these past three years. But I'm not going to give you credit for the idea. I was way ahead of you…. Ow! Damn it, Amanda. That *did* hurt."

"I know you better than you think I do." And with that, she rose to her feet, gave me one of those "don't you wish?" looks, and walked slowly back to the water, swinging her hips as she went, the pink bikini bottom barely hanging to her amazing….

Wow. Talking about getting lucky.

I jumped to my feet and ran after her. She heard me coming and headed out into deeper water, took a header into the surf, and began a strong crawl away from the shore, and damn it, I couldn't catch her. I hadn't realized what a strong swimmer she was.

I gave up and waited, treading water. Finally, she flipped over onto her back and waved.

"Come on, Harry. Don't be a baby. You can do it."

Do it? Sure I could, but I wasn't about to give her the satisfaction. I turned to swim leisurely back toward the resort, and that's when I realized how far out we were. At least a hundred yards, probably more, and the distance was increasing. Riptide.

Oh shit.

I turned and looked at Amanda. She was now in rough water, and I could barely see her head bobbing above the waves. I began to swim hard toward her, and a couple of minutes later I felt the pain in my arm start searing through the muscle. And soon it was me that was in trouble. I could no longer see her, and I all but panicked. I treaded water, looked wildly around; I couldn't see her. Where was she? I felt my stomach tighten. I splashed around for what seemed like an hour, but it could only have been five, maybe ten minutes. My damned arm was virtually useless, I still couldn't see her, and I was struggling to stay afloat. *Oh shit. Oh my God. Where the hell is she?*

"Stop it, Harry," she shouted in my ear.

Oh thank God.

"Where the hell did you come from?" I shouted.

"Stop thrashing around. Be still. Relax. Turn over. On your back. Use your legs. Take deep breaths and hold them as long as you can. It will help you float."

I felt her slide underneath me. Her hands went under my armpits.

"This way. Just take it easy. Let me handle it. We're going this way."

For five, maybe ten minutes, we swam—no, she swam, with me in tow, parallel to the shore, and then we turned for home. It must have taken thirty minutes for us to reach water shallow enough for us both to stand, and by the time we did I could tell she was exhausted.

She let go of me and flopped down on her back in the crystal clear, but oh-so-deadly water, floating, breathing heavily.

"What the hell happened out there, and where the hell did you learn to do that?" I gasped, on my knees beside her.

"Do what?"

"You swim like a fish. I couldn't see you. You'd disappeared. I thought you had drowned."

"Not on your life. I only just snagged you."

"No, Amanda. Seriously. I thought I'd lost you. I was coming for you, and then I couldn't move my arm anymore. I…."

She looked at me, smiled, and whispered, "I went out too far. I tried to get back, but the current was too strong, so I swam parallel to the shore until I could no longer feel it, then I turned in toward shore…. I… I could see you were in trouble, so… I swam toward shore until I was sure I could come up behind you. It didn't take a genius to figure it out."

I put my arms around her, pulled her to me, and kissed the tip of her nose, her eyelids, each cheek, and finally her lips. "Thank you. I don't think I could have made it back on my own."

She stood, took my hand, and said, "Well. Let's go in. I need to look at your arm."

"Okay, but don't say anything, especially to my father and Rose. They have enough on their minds right now with Henry. They don't need to be worrying about me."

My left forearm was a mess. The wounds hadn't opened; they were well healed. The interior workings—artery and bone—were not. From my elbow to my wrist, my arm had swelled up like a damned balloon.

Amanda took my hand, looked at it, looked up at me, her eyes watering, and said, "Oh my God. That's not good, Harry. Please tell me I didn't do that when I punched you."

"You didn't. I promise. It was my shoulder you punched."

"We need to get you to a doctor. I'll get a towel and make an ice pack."

Hell, she was right. The look of the thing put the fear of God into me. *Shit, I could lose my damned arm. Who's the doctor?*

"Get my phone," I said when she returned. "It's in the bedroom. Call Jane Matheson. She's a gynecologist, but I think she's the only doctor on the island. Her number's in the list."

She made the call and caught the doctor on her lunch break. Matheson told us to go right on over to her clinic, she would join us there, and so that was what we did.

Three hours, a little blood work, and an X-ray later, we were back in the cottage. Fortunately, the white cell count was normal, so there was no infection, and there was no new damage to the artery. The stent was still in place and there was no internal bleeding; the wound had simply become inflamed due to overexertion. Ice, a mild antibiotic, and a little ibuprofen, and I'd be back in shape soon, so she said. She had also offered a prescription painkiller, but I turned that down.

Amanda and I spent the rest of the day together on the private patio at the rear of the cottage. By the time we were called to dinner, the swelling had gone down enough that it attracted neither attention nor unwanted questions. It was the end of a day I was glad to see the back of, and one I was sure I would never forget.

Chapter 23

Amanda and I spent the next several days doing what newlywed couples do when on their honeymoons, and I played a couple rounds of golf with my dad and Bob. August won, as usual, and took great delight in relieving each of us of a twenty-dollar bill. For a man who was almost a billionaire, he took a childish delight in winning such small sums. It was the same when he played poker—he was a master at that too. He never played for more than a two-dollar ante, and he always came out ahead. Me? I avoided poker like the plague. The principles—bluff and observation—I used as tools in my work as an investigator and interrogator; the game I steered clear of.

The early mornings were pure bliss. We stayed in bed late, drank copious amounts of expensive coffee, and... well, we made love like there was no tomorrow. After almost three years, I thought I knew the woman. But during those three days I found out that I'd barely scratched the surface. She was caring, attentive, loving, and every moment I spent with her was a learning experience—for her too, I'm sure.

Bliss those days might have been, but lurking somewhere never very far from the surface of my subconscious was the riddle that was the Martan family murder. Time and again, at

197

the most inopportune moments, it would break through and, like a cold hand at the scruff of my neck, drag me back to the real world.

Early that Friday afternoon, it happened again. We were still at lunch. Bob and Kate were off somewhere together. Tim and Sammie were at another table huddled together over a laptop, Jacque and Wendy were poolside, and my dad and Rose had just left to take a nap.

"What on earth is going on in there?" Amanda asked.

I snapped back to reality with a jerk. "What? What do you mean?"

"Where were you, Harry? You certainly weren't with me."

I shrugged. "I was away with the birds, up at the Martan home, trying to make some sense of what we know.... No, it's what we don't know that I can't get a handle on. We have no physical evidence. Nothing to tie anyone to the scene. I also think we're missing something. I think we need to get the forensics people back and have her room gone over again. I'll organize that right now. Just hang tight while I do."

I flipped the screen on my iPhone and dialed Daisy Patel's number.

She answered on the second ring.

"Ms. Patel? How is your daughter? Is everything okay?"

"Yes. She has a little girl. They're both doing fine."

"That's wonderful. Congratulations on your first grandchild."

"…What do you need, Mr. Starke? I know you didn't call to ask about my daughter."

"Actually, I did…. Well, I would have, but look, I have a couple of questions. First: Is there any word on the blood spot you found on the carpet in Gabrielle's room?"

"No, I'm afraid not. And I suspect it will take at least a couple more weeks to get the results of the DNA analysis. We won't know for sure if it's the victim's or someone else's until then. Sorry."

That wasn't good news. I needed to know if the blood belonged to the killer. If so, it would be just a matter of running DNA comparisons. *Hell, I'd better have Tommy get samples anyway.*

"Okay. I'll have to live with that. In the meantime, I want Gabrielle Martan's rooms gone over again, and I'd like it done as quickly as possible. My time here on the island is limited. Killers, as we both know, always either leave something behind or take something away; I'm thinking the blood, but there may be something else we're missing. For instance, what the hell did the killer hit her with? If it wasn't premeditated, it would have been something he or she found handy in that room, and then took away with them. Can you come back and do that for me, please?"

"Well I can, of course, but I was going to call you anyway. Listen. You know we vacuumed the carpets in her rooms? They were very clean, probably because the maid does them every day, but we did find a lot of debris deep down in the pile. Most of it was just the usual stuff produced by everyday living, but there were also three chips of white glass, old glass, milk glass. Two of them are tiny, almost microscopic, and one slightly larger...."

"*Yes*! That's what I'm talking about. That's it. I knew it. I knew there had to be something. Stay with your daughter, Ms. Patel. If there's anything else, I'll call you." In my excitement, I hung up without saying goodbye. *Damn! So maybe the blood* does *belong to the killer. If whatever it was broke in his hand....*

I called her back, apologized, and disconnected again, feeling more than a little stupid. And then I called Tommy and asked him to take mouth swabs from everyone connected to the house. Kate's phone went straight to voicemail; she must have been out somewhere with Bob, because I couldn't get hold of him either. I did get a hold of Michael Collins at the resort office and arrange to use one the courtesy vehicles. Finally, I called Leo Martan Sr., told him I would be there within the hour, and asked him to meet me.

He wasn't happy, but he said he would.

Chapter 24

"Mr. Martan," I said as I climbed the steps to the front entrance. "I need to take another look at Gabrielle's rooms, and I need you to go with me. You know them, their layout, and you knew your daughter better than anyone else, or at least I assume you did." I paused, waited for him to answer. He didn't. He simply nodded, and then turned and led the way into the house.

"I need you to check and see if anything's missing," I said, as we stood before the open door; the tape was still in place. "In particular, I'd like you to check the milk glass. There's a lot of it."

"I'm not the person to do that," he said. "My wife, though. She visited Gabrielle now and then. Not so much these last few weeks. They've been at odds just lately. Let me call her."

He fished his iPhone from his pants pocket and made the call. We didn't have to wait long. Vivien was in the suite next door with Alicia.

"Mrs. Martan," I said when she joined us, "please put these on." I handed her a pair of Tyvek over-booties. "I'd like you to check the milk glass. I think there may be a piece missing."

She slipped the over-booties on, and so did I, and together we stepped into the living room; Leo stayed outside in the hall.

202

She glanced around the room, went into the bedroom, spent less than thirty seconds there, and then returned, shaking her head.

"There's nothing missing," she said, but I knew by the tone of her voice that there was.

What the hell?

"Yes there is," Martan said suddenly from the hallway. "One of the glass bottles is missing. I can see it from here. The biggest one from the coffee table. I know because I remember you buying it when we were in Charleston. You gave it to her for her collection."

"Oh that. That was years ago," she said sharply. "It must be here somewhere. It's not in the bedroom. Maybe she put it away with the other extra pieces."

"Can you describe it to me?" I asked.

"I can do better than that." She flipped the lock screen on her iPhone, flipping through several screens until she found the one she was looking for.

"I think you mean this one, the tall, square one," she said to Leo, showing him the phone.

"Yes, that's it."

She handed me the phone.

The photo showed the coffee table with a group of six white bottles of varying sizes. I looked from the photo to the table; there were only five there now. Sure enough, one was missing. Judging by the size of those remaining, I estimated it to be perhaps ten inches tall including the neck, which was about three inches long. The body of the bottle was a rectangle, maybe seven inches by two by three. In the photo it was indeed the tallest of the group, if not the largest, and the neck protruded above the rest—easy to grab in the heat of the moment.

"When did you take this?" I asked, watching her face. "When was the last time you saw it, do you remember?"

She didn't hesitate. "The photo? Oh a couple of months ago, I suppose, maybe more. I haven't seen the bottle since. She probably moved it. Maybe she swapped it out with one of her other pieces."

What was that look?

"You're sure it was that long ago?"

"Of course."

"Please think again, Mrs. Martan. It could be important."

"I don't need to. I'm sure."

"How?"

She looked away and then shook her head, exasperated. "Because, as Leo said, I gave it to her. I was always on the lookout for new pieces for her. I bought that one more than a year ago, and it wasn't in Charleston. It was in Atlanta. She must have moved it. That's all. She was always arranging and rearranging her milk glass, bringing in new pieces, taking pieces out, trying for a different look. It was an obsession with her. There are boxes and boxes of the stuff in the basement. She brings—I mean she brought—pieces up; she took pieces down."

I didn't believe her for a second. She couldn't even look me in the eye. I held out my hand. "Can I see your phone for a minute?"

"You most certainly may not. I have all sorts of private things on it."

"Oh, I just want to take a look at the photograph, that's all."

"I'll hold it," she said, stepping closer to me.

She held the iPhone up for me to see. I squinted, leaned closer, playacting. I could see perfectly well. I reached out with my right hand and took hold of her wrist, drew it toward my face, and then winced as pain shot up my arm as I tapped the back arrow with the forefinger of my left hand. She tried to snatch her hand away, but I held on. The screen changed to reveal half a dozen thumbnails, one of which was the photo of the coffee table.

"Oh look," I said. "You took several photos of her rooms that day. Why was that?"

"She was rearranging things. She wanted my opinion on how things looked. I took photos for her."

"Hmmm." I looked her right in the eye. "And would you just look at the date," I said thoughtfully. "November 10. That was only ten days ago. Why did you lie to me, Mrs. Martan?"

"I did not lie to you," she said hotly. "I merely got confused over the date. I have a very busy life. If I don't write things down, I forget them."

"You didn't forget taking the photographs," I said gently.

Her face was white. She looked at Leo for help. She got none.

"I was confused about the date. That's all. Anyway. What difference does it make? So it was there on the table less than two weeks ago. So what? She moved it. It's probably down in the basement with rest of the collection."

"Would you mind if I took a look?" I asked her.

"No... not at all."

She's not too gung-ho about the idea. What is *she hiding?*

"I'll have Moore take you down there," Leo said.

"I'll go with you," she said quickly.

The basement was a warren of unfinished rooms, most of them still separated by unfinished, open-stud walls, but that didn't mean it was empty; far from it. Furniture was piled everywhere. Long rolls of carpets, gym equipment, pool equipment, skis, canoes, and stacks and stacks of cardboard boxes.

"Miss Gabrielle's things are over here," Moore said, leading the way. And they were indeed. Dozens of cardboard boxes, some full of clothes, some of shoes, or schoolbooks, or glassware, all piled one atop another. The milk-glass collection consisted of five huge boxes full of the stuff, each piece carefully wrapped in white tissue paper.

"I need to get some help," I said. "I need to make a call."

"I'll help," Moore said quietly. "We're looking for a bottle, right? Can I see the photo please, so I know what we're looking for?"

Vivien showed him the photo and then the three of us got work. Yep, she helped too.

It took a while, but between us we unwrapped every piece of milk glass in all five boxes. There were literally hundreds of pieces. The one we were looking for? You guessed it. It wasn't there.

I sighed, looked at the hundreds of pieces of glassware spread out over every flat surface, including the floor. I didn't envy the person who had rewrap it all, but it sure wasn't going to be me.

"I need you to send that photo to my iPhone," I told Vivien. "Please do it now."

I waited until I had the image safely on my phone, and then I left them to it, returned to the

207

foyer, and called Leo Martan. He was in his office.

Before I joined him, however, I made a call to the USVI Police Headquarters and spoke for several minutes to Chief Walker. I explained what was going on, and my theory, and then I made a request to which he readily acquiesced. And then I joined Martan.

"We didn't find that bottle, or what's left of it." I told him. "I'm certain it was the weapon used to hit your daughter in the head. I'm also certain that it broke under the impact. The CSI team found shards of broken milk glass in the carpet, which is why I'm here. I need you to keep that information to yourself. Don't mention it to anyone, including your wife. Is that clear, sir?"

"Of course. What do you intend to do now?"

"I've arranged for a dozen officers to be flown in here from Charlotte Amalie—the first group will be arriving by helicopter very soon. When they get here, I'll have them search every inch of this house. I need to find that bottle. It could have fingerprints on it."

He nodded. "Is there anything I can do?"

"Yes," I said. "I need for you to tell everyone here that they must cooperate with the officers, and stay in their rooms until the search is complete. I do not want anyone…." And then I had a thought. "No, actually, just tell them to cooperate." *With a bit of luck, we'll flush someone out. If there are fingerprints on the bottle, the perp will know it, and go after it. Well, maybe. It's worth a shot. The only trouble is keeping watch on them all. Well, not all. Just....*

"I need to ask you a question, Mr. Martan. Why did your wife lie about when the photo of the bottle was taken?"

"Did she lie? I don't think she did. She's forgetful, gets confused. I don't think she lied."

"Let me tell you what I think," I said. "I think she lied because she was covering for her daughter, Alicia. I think she thinks that Alicia killed Gabrielle, probably in revenge for the affair with her husband. Or maybe she thought that your daughter was about to take him away from her altogether. That would be a severe blow, to Alicia's lifestyle, her finances, and her ego—lots of motive, opportunity for sure, and the means: the bottle." I watched him carefully as I continued. "Either that, or your wife killed her."

"What? That's ridiculous. What possible motive—"

"For the same reason. To protect her daughter from the humiliation and inevitable losses a divorce would bring. It's a strong motive: a mother protecting her child. She also had means and opportunity. Either way, she was lying. I knew it, and so—did—you!"

He looked at me, uncomfortably, and then he looked away.

209

"My God…. You think so too!"

He looked at me. His face was a mask. He didn't answer.

"You do, don't you?" I asked. "Which one? Your wife, or her daughter?"

Again, there was no answer. He simply put his elbows on the desk, steepled his fingers against his lips, and stared at me. I waited for him to say something.

Finally, he leaned back in his chair, let his hands fall to his lap, and said, "I don't know. Vivien's been on edge lately. It was common knowledge… about Gabrielle and Jeffery. Everyone knew. Yes, I know what I said, but I knew too. There was talk about him leaving Alicia for Gabrielle, but that's all it was: talk. I knew it wouldn't happen; I knew Gab too well. When she was killed, my first thought was Leo, then Alicia, but as the days passed, I began to suspect Vivien as well, that they might have done it together. Look. It's only suspicion. I have no real grounds for it. It's just that I know them all so well, which is why I insisted on having you carry out the investigation. Now you're thinking what I'm thinking…. It's—it's unbearable."

Faintly, but growing louder, I began to hear the deep *whump-whump-whump* of an approaching helicopter. The lead elements of the search team were here. I left Leo to pass on the word to the family that they were to cooperate, and I went out to meet the helicopter. Tommy Quinn was the first to step off the aircraft.

I filled him in, had him deploy three of his four officers, gave them their instructions, and then I had him and the fourth member of his team stand by with me. Between us, we would watch for any errant family or staff member who might decide to go after the bottle. It was a bit of a Hail Mary, but it was all I had, because not for a single moment did I think we would find the bottle. And I was right. We didn't. Nor did we catch anyone going after it. Whoever had done it must have been pretty damn confident that either we wouldn't find it or, if we did, that it wouldn't matter.

The chopper had arrived just after two thirty. It went back for a second load and returned forty-five minutes later. We now had ten officers on the ground, searching the house. And search it they did. Big as it was, from my own observations, I think they missed nothing, nor did any member of the family or staff, either by expression or action, give any hint of the location of that damned bottle.

By ten o'clock that evening, they were all on their way back St. Thomas. Me? I was so pissed off I could barely contain myself. Not only that; my arm was giving me hell. I was hurting, and in more ways than one.

When I arrived back at the resort, it was almost eleven o'clock. I was tired, irritable, hungry, and in need of a kind word and a stiff drink. Fortunately, Amanda had shrimp-salad sandwiches made, a half tumbler of Laphroaig with a single cube of ice, a soothing hand for my weary brow, a great many kind words, and the bed already turned down. And suddenly, I felt a whole lot better.

Chapter 25

The following morning, I was up early. Hell, I'd been up most of the night. Despite two large measures of my favorite Scottish drink, I couldn't sleep. My arm was hurting and I couldn't get what Leo Martan Sr. had said out of my mind. I needed to run it by the crew.

Over breakfast, I did just that. I related what Leo Sr. and I had talked about the previous evening, and I asked for opinions.

"So let me get this straight," Kate said, frowning. "You think that Vivien thinks that Alicia killed Gabrielle and removed the bottle. You also think that Alicia thinks her mother did it and that she, Alicia, removed the bottle. And to complicate things even more, old man Martan thinks they were both involved, that one or the other did it, or that they did it together. Is that correct?"

"Pretty much. It kinda makes sense, don't you think?"

"It does," Kate said, "but I'll muddy the waters a little more: yes, it's a good little basket of theories, but I think Jeffery might be involved too. Suppose she did dump him. We know from Leo Jr.'s statement that Gabrielle argued with one of them that morning. Jeffery says it was him but it could have been... eh, whatever. He could have gone to see her that morning. Maybe they argued some more; maybe he lost it, grabbed the bottle, hit her with it, panicked, called his wife... oh hell, I don't know."

I grinned at her. "Now you see why I didn't sleep last night. Whatever. I'm thinking it was either Vivien or Alicia."

Slowly, she shook her head. "Man, I don't know. It's a hell of a stretch, but... maybe."

But I was wrong, and was soon proved to be so.

It was just after ten o'clock that morning. We'd finished breakfast and were all on the patio enjoying the early morning sunshine, which was tempered by a light ocean breeze.

I still had the case at the forefront of my mind—it's who I am—but other than mull things over and hope for the lights to turn themselves on, there was little, other than that damned bottle, that was new information. Tommy Quinn was, I thought, back in Charlotte Amalie on St. Thomas, and all was peaceful—until my phone vibrated on the glass top of the table.

"Harry?" It was Quinn. "I need you back up at the Mount, soon as you can. Alicia Margolis is dead. It looks like suicide. Dr. Wilson, the ME, is on his way over from St. Thomas and should have arrived by the time you get here."

For a moment I didn't say anything. I was stunned, flabbergasted, dumbfounded, buffaloed, gobsmacked; all of those and more. All of my theories had just gone out the window. Maybe

214

literally. My mind was a total blank, but I told him I could and would be there, then I disconnected and slammed my phone down on the table. What I wanted to do was throw the damned thing in the pool.

"*Friggin' hell*," I all but shouted. I would have said something a whole lot stronger had my father and Rose not been seated right next to me.

"What?" Amanda asked. "What's wrong?"

"Alicia friggin' Margolis is what's wrong. She's killed herself. Sorry Amanda, folks. I gotta go. Kate?"

She nodded. "I'll be right back. I need to change first."

"Bob. There's no need for you to come. It shouldn't take long."

"That's okay. I'll stay here with your folks."

Ten minutes later, Kate and I were on our way to the resort office to find Michael Collins to see about getting a ride to the house.

We found him in his office, told him what we needed, but not why, and once again he agreed to let us use one of the resort's courtesy cars.

Tommy Quinn, along with both Leos, Vivien Martan—her eyes and face bloated from crying—Moore, and Jeffery Margolis were waiting for us when we arrived some twenty minutes after ten; the ME was still on his way. Leo wanted to take us right on up to the Margolises' suite, but I insisted we wait for Dr. Wilson.

"Where is she, exactly?" I asked.

It was Jeffery Margolis who answered. "In... in the bathroom," he managed, his face white, his hands shaking. "She... she... she's in the bath. She cu... cu... her wrists, she...."

"You went into the bathroom, right?"

He nodded.

"Who else?" I asked, mentally crossing my fingers.

"I went in," Martan said. "But only as far as the door, and I didn't touch anything. I got him—" he nodded at Jeffery "—out of there and locked the door. No one else has been inside."

I nodded, and inwardly heaved a sigh of relief.

We didn't have to wait long. In the distance I heard the thumping of a helicopter's rotors, the noise growing louder as it drew closer. We walked around the house and watched it set down next to Leo's machine, and Dr. Wilson, accompanied by Daisy Patel and someone else I'd never seen before, stepped out. The unknown man was carrying a large cardboard box.

The box contained several sets of Tyvek coveralls. We suited up and put on latex gloves in the hallway outside the Margolises' suite. While we were doing so, I couldn't help but notice the faint traces of blood in the door opening and down the hall.

Not good, I thought. *Not good at all. Jeff Margolis, for sure, and he's contaminated the scene.*

I was impressed with Wilson. I'd talked to him on the phone; in person he was, however, not at all what I'd expected. He was a very thin man, about five foot ten with a great shock of white hair and a white toothbrush mustache—and he was all business.

The bathroom was huge, with a walk-in steam shower, a second walk-in shower stall with a multi-jet rainfall system, two vanities, two white leather chairs, and an ornate, free-standing bathtub. Alicia Margolis, dressed only in a bra and panties, lay semi-submerged in the tub. The water was bright red and almost at the rim. Her left hand was underwater. Her right lay across her breasts at surface level. There was a serrated steak knife lying on the floor beside the tub; there was blood on the blade, and what I took to be arterial spray all around the right side of the tub. And there were footprints, what looked to be a man's footprints. *Jeffery's? Probably.*

We stood back and waited while Daisy Patel took photographs, then Wilson leaned over the tub and lifted Alicia's right hand. Sure enough there was a deep gash across her wrist, almost to the bone, from what I could see. He laid it back down, walked around the tub, and fished in the bloody water for her left arm. He pulled it up, looked at it—I looked at it—then he looked at me and nodded.

"Do you mind, Harry?" he asked, indicating her right hand with his head.

217

I stepped forward, picking my way carefully through the blood spatters, and lifted her right hand. Together we looked back and forth, first at one, then the other, comparing the cuts. I laid her hand back on her breast and stepped away.

"It's not suicide, is it," I said. "Even I can see that. Both cuts were made from left to right, and both are angled the same way: up the arm from the base of the palm in the case of the right hand, and from the base of the thumb on the left. Both are right-handed cuts. You can't cut your own right wrist with your own right hand. Not only that; if I'm correct, the cut to her right wrist is so deep it must have cut the tendons. In which case, the hand would have been rendered useless and she wouldn't have been able to make the second cut."

"Very impressive, Harry. Right in every respect. No, this was a homicide, no doubt about it, and a clumsy one at that."

Jeffy-baby, I thought. *But why? Hmmm. Perhaps not.*

"Time of death, Doc?"

He looked sharply at me, obviously not happy with the term of address.

I tilted my sideways and shrugged. "Sorry, habit. Doctor."

He nodded once, looked down at the corpse, put his hand in the water, and swished it around.

"Hard to say. The water's room temperature. I'll take her body temperature when we get her out, but I don't think it will help. Eight to fourteen hours would be my best guess. I'll be able to give you a better estimate once I've done the post, and analyzed the contents of her stomach. Until then…."

I nodded and left him to it. I stopped at the bathroom door, checked for a clean area of floor, removed the booties, and stepped onto it. I leaned out through the doorframe and saw Kate checking out the living room.

"Hey," I said. "Would you mind getting me some fresh booties, please?"

She did, and I put them on, bagged and labeled those I'd just removed, set them aside for forensics, and then joined her in the living room.

"And?" she asked.

"Homicide. The killer tried to set it up to look like a suicide. Poor job. Might even be the break we were looking for. We'll see. You find anything yet?"

"Not much of anything out of place. There are those." She pointed to an almost-empty bottle of red wine and an empty wineglass on the coffee table in front of the sofa.

I knelt down beside the table, leaned over the glass, and sniffed.

"Chlorine," I said. "The odor's weak, but it's there…. That probably means ketamine. She was drugged." I looked around. Daisy was in the kitchen doing something I couldn't see.

"Hey Ms. Patel," I called.

"Mr. Starke," she said as she joined us in the living room.

"I need you to dust this glass and the bottle for prints, please, and there's a knife on the bathroom floor. I need that done too, but you'll probably need to wait for the ME to finish before you can get in there. Also, there's a lot of blood on the floor, in the bathroom and out in the hall. The killer had to have gotten some of it on his shoes. We know Jeffery Margolis has been in there—he found the body—but check to see if there are any other shoe prints…. What?"

"You don't need to be telling me how to do my job, Mr. Starke. Now, if you'll get out of the way, I'll dust the glass and bottle for you."

"Oh, hell, Daisy. I'm sorry. I didn't—"

"Think? I know. Now please move."

I moved. It took her just a few seconds to dust the two items.

"Nothing on the bottle. Looks like a thumb, forefinger, and two fingertips on the glass."

"See what I mean?" I asked Kate. "The bottle's been wiped, but not the glass. Whoever did it obviously didn't touch the glass, but the bottle…. That wasn't too smart. And only one glass…. Hmmm. If she'd had company, surely she wouldn't have drank alone… would she have…? Wait. I need to check something."

I went into the kitchen. There was nothing on the draining board.

I opened the cupboard over the sink. There was a wine glass rack attached to the inside of the top; you know the type of thing: several rows of slits where you slide the stems of the glasses in and they hang upside down.

"She had company," I said over my shoulder. "There's a glass out of place in here. The stem is slightly longer. It should go here." I pointed. "It's the only one out of place. Daisy, I need you to dust it, if you would, please." She did. There was nothing. The glass had been washed and wiped clean. I smiled.

"Why would the killer wash one glass but not the other?" Kate asked.

"Probably to make us think Alicia was drinking on her own, got drunk, and decided to kill herself."

"And wiped the bottle and washed the glass," Kate said, nodding.

"Yeah. As I said, not too smart."

I walked through to the bathroom. Wilson was on his knees by the tub, mumbling into a recorder. He stopped when he saw me at the door.

"Can I grab the knife?" I asked.

He nodded and, taking extra care to avoid the blood, I stepped over the tiled floor and picked the knife up by the tip of the blade, and then returned to the living room.

"Here," I said, handing the knife to Daisy Patel.

"No," she said. "Just hold it up. Yes, just like that."

I was holding the point in my fingertips. She dusted the handle.

"Yes!" she said brightly. "I see one, two, three, four perfect prints."

"Perfect?" I asked. "That never happens. One, even two, maybe, but four?" I shook my head. I looked at Kate. "You wanna bet they all belong to Alicia?"

She smiled, at the same time slowly shaking her head. "You're not suggesting someone placed them there, are you?" she asked sarcastically.

"Uhhh, yeah!"

Daisy carefully took the knife from me and placed it in a paper evidence bag, being careful not to disturb the blood.

"When?" I asked.

"Give me thirty minutes. I need to go to the chopper and get my gear. I'll lift and scan them, and give you a copy of the file."

"Great. And please do the glass too. I'll have Tim run comparisons, but we all know damn well who they belong to."

"How long will it take you and your buddy to process the suite and hall?" I asked Daisy.

She looked at her watch. "It's almost eleven thirty now. I doubt we'll get done with it today. Not unless we work all... night?" She looked sideways at me, her head tilted, her eyes wide, questioning. I looked back at her and shrugged.

"Okay," she sighed. "You got it. Okay if I wake you up when I'm done?"

I grinned at her. "Not hardly."

"Yeah, right. Go on; get out of here. I need to get to work."

"Ok… ay," I said. In the middle of it, I had another thought. I picked up the wine glass by its stem, waved it under my nose, breathed deeply, and handed it to her.

"Daisy," I said. "It smells like chlorine. Ketamine, right?"

She raised the glass to her nose, closed her eyes, and breathed in, slowly. She took her time about it, but eventually she nodded. "I can't be absolutely sure, but yes, I think so. I'll test it, along with everything else I have to do…. By the way," she said sweetly, "would you like me to stick a broom up my ass and sweep up as I go?"

"Whatever you think will get the job done," I said, just as sweetly.

"Hah."

Kate and I went out into the hall and stripped off the Tyvek coveralls.

"Let's go see if there's coffee in the dining room," I said.

Chapter 26

Coffee there was aplenty, so we each grabbed a cup and then went out onto the patio and sat down. The view was, as always, breathtaking. *One of these days, maybe....*

"So what do we have?" Kate asked, lifting her feet up onto the chair next to her.

"Well first of all I think we can say that neither Alicia nor Vivien killed Gabrielle. True, Alicia's death doesn't completely rule Vivien out, but if she did kill Gabby, why? I'm damned sure that Vivien wouldn't murder her own daughter. So someone else killed her and, by default, Alicia too. Once again, though, there's very little physical evidence, and I doubt there will be. Maybe footprints, if we get lucky, but I'm not holding my breath. Reality TV has a lot to answer for. You?"

She thought for a moment. "I don't think there's any doubt that both were killed by the same person, but why...."

"Oh, I think we know that."

"Oh? Do tell."

"Whoever killed them was, I think, a little too smart for their own good: wiping the wine bottle, washing the second glass, planting the fingerprints on the knife; those were all stupid mistakes a four-year-old wouldn't have made. Whoever killed Alicia did so to divert attention

224

away from himself, to make it look like Alicia killed Gabrielle and then, in a fit of either remorse or fear of discovery, killed herself. It might have worked, but for the obvious mistakes. Alicia and her mother were my prime suspects. Her killer effectively eliminated them both from the list."

"So, you have a list of suspects," she said over the rim of her cup. "Are you going to share it with me?"

"Maybe," I grinned at her. "What about you? Who do you think it was? And don't say the damned butler."

She smiled at me. "But I do like the butler for it, at least for this one. Think about it. Didn't he tell you if he found out who killed Gabby, he'd take care of it? And he was screwing Gabby...."

"We don't know that for sure."

"Yes we do. Well I do. I've seen the look he had on his face before, on someone else, *haven't I* Harry."

"Yeah," I said, ignoring her obvious innuendo. "We both have, many times. Maybe he was; maybe he wasn't. He was certainly fond of her...."

"He was having an affair with her, Harry. It was obvious. And, well... I know. I just know."

"Okay," I said. "Let's assume, just for a moment, that he was. Why would he kill her?"

"For any one of half a dozen reasons I can think of right off the top of my head. The most obvious being, she wasn't taking him seriously."

"Oh?"

225

"Sure. I think he would have liked to marry her; but she didn't want to marry him. A lowly servant? She wouldn't go for that, would she? So it's simple. They had a falling out. He lost his temper. Whack. He thinks he's killed her and dumps her over the balcony."

"Nope. I don't think so. Moore is ex-special forces. He'd know she wasn't dead. Not only that; if he had hit her, he *would* have killed her. He's a tough son of a bitch."

"Well," she said, "there's that, I suppose. So come on, give. Who do you like for it?"

"There are three, actually…."

"Hey, hang on, something just hit me. What about Georgina? She was having it off with Alicia. Maybe she killed her…. Jealousy? Now Alicia's dead, she has no alibi for Gabby's TOD."

"Sheesh." I sucked air in through my teeth. "That would be a stretch. I don't see that. I think Alicia was in love with her."

She looked quizzically at me over the rim of her cup.

"As I was saying, I have three suspects: I moved Leo Jr. to the top of the list. He's the one with the most to gain. He'll grab something like fourteen million. I've known people to kill for less than fourteen dollars, and so have you. Then there's Alicia's husband, Jeffery. He was in love with Gabrielle, and he hated his wife. More good motives…."

"No, Harry. That one I'm not buying. Leo, maybe, but not Jeff. Yes, he could have killed

Gabrielle, but I don't think so, because if the killings are linked, he must have planned the second one. Think about it. He had to get hold of the drug. Ketamine's not something you can get off the shelf at the local pharmacy. That's premeditation…. Wait. Didn't Leo Jr. mention something about Miami? Ketamine would be easy to get on the street there. Maybe he…." She shook her head, clucked her tongue against the roof of her mouth, thinking, and then she continued. "It fits. He, Leo, is not too swift in the head. He drugged her and calmly cut her wrists. Did you see the depth of those cuts? Jeff's a wimp. He doesn't have it in him to kill like that, not anyone, let alone his wife, for God's sake. So yeah, Leo. Who else ya got?"

"The pirate captain?"

"Carriere was on his boat."

"He *said* he was on his boat. And even if he really was, it's just a short walk, or run, from the dock to the side entrance of the house, five minutes each way at the most. He'd only need to be away from the boat for thirty minutes, with a little bit of luck, to do the deed and get back. A little bit of luck…. We need to find out what he was doing last night. Eight to fourteen hours, Wilson said, that would have put her time of death sometime between eight in the evening—but I'd guess it was later than that—and two in the morning. We need to find out where he was."

"We can do that, but what about the other two?"

"Let's go find out," I said, setting my cup down and getting to my feet.

We found Jeffery Margolis in the living room, watching Fox News.

"Just the man we're looking for," I said, dumping myself down onto the sofa beside him. "So tell me." I was done wasting time on the niceties. I wanted to get out of there and get back to living my new life. "Where were you, Jeffery, between eight last night and two this morning?"

"I was asleep, in one of the spare rooms, in the east wing. She threw me out...."

"So you have no alibi?" I said, getting up again.

"I... I... I...."

"Oh forget it," I said. "Where can I find Leo Jr.?"

"I haven't seen him. But he's probably upstairs, in his office. He almost always is."

"What are you doing?" Kate asked as I headed for the stairs. "That was no interview."

"Yep, it was. He has no alibi. That's all I need to know for right now. There's nothing more we can do until Daisy is finished processing the Margolises' rooms and we get the results, except try to establish alibis. I did that, and he ain't got one. And neither, I bet, does his ever-lovin' stepbrother-in-law."

And I was right. He didn't. His wife, Lucy, had also tossed him out after a screaming match about money. She wanted some, and he didn't have any, and wouldn't ask his father. He'd spent the night on the Chesterfield sofa in his office.

"What now?" Kate asked, as we descended the stairs and walked out into the foyer.

"I want to go see Sebastian Carriere. I think a ride down to the docks is in order. I also want to see how easy it would be for him to get to the house from there, on foot."

Sebastian Carriere was on his boat when we arrived at the docks. I could see him doing something on the flying bridge as I wandered toward his berth.

"Kate," I said quietly, so as not to be heard, "go wander around the docks. Check with the other boat owners. See if the boat was here yesterday. More to the point, see if you can find out if *he* was here."

She stuck her hands in the pockets of her shorts and wandered off, stopping here and there to admire the boats.

"Mr. Starke," he called down, leaning over the rail so that he could see me. "I thought you'd never get here. Is that the lovely lieutenant I see over there? What's she doing, checking my alibi? Well, good luck with that. They're a closed-mouth bunch around here. You want to come aboard and chat a little, or have you come to arrest me?"

"I have no power to arrest you," I said, "but I will come aboard."

"And so you shall, me hearty. So you shall."

Jeez, enough with the Long John Silver impersonations already.

The boat was a forty-eight-foot Riviera sport fisherman named *Gabby II*.

What, I wondered, *happened to* Gabby I*?*

Now I didn't know anything about boats, at least not then, but just looking at this one I could see at least half a million dollars.

I stepped aboard, and Carriere held out his left hand for me to shake—*hmmm, left handed, okay.* I took it with my right hand—awkward to do—and immediately became involved in a test of strength. He was strong and fit, but he was no match for me, and I watched his smile melt away when I stepped up the pressure. It was over in a heartbeat, and he turned quickly and led the way to a table at the stern.

"Please, sit," he said. I did. "What can I do for you, Mr. Starke?"

It was at that moment I realized I didn't like this man. There was something about his attitude, his demeanor, but mostly it was his eyes. They were almost black, like a snake's. They put me in no mood for social niceties.

"Where were you last night between eight and two this morning?"

He tilted his head, narrowed his eyes. "Here, on the boat. Why?"

230

"You haven't heard?"

"Heard what?"

"Alicia Margolis was murdered last night. Can you prove you were here all night?" I watched his eyes—not a flicker.

"Alicia's dead? God. I can't prove anything, no. Randy, my deck hand, was here until just after ten, but after he left.... I wasn't feeling too good, so I went to bed."

"How did you get along with Mrs. Margolis?"

He frowned. "What do you mean? I didn't. I didn't know her. Well, I'd met her, but that was about it. That woman and her husband move and live in a different world. You did notice that I'm not white, right?"

I knew what he meant; I also knew he had issues about his race. I *also* knew that he was right; the likes of the Martan family did not mix with the lower classes, much less when those people were of a different ethnicity.

I nodded, rose from my seat, and made to leave. I stopped at the rail and turned. "Nice view of the house," I said.

The smile he gave me was tinged with sarcasm, and so was his reply.

"True," he said. "And what you're hinting at is also true. It's an easy five-minute walk from here to the side entrance. I've done it many times;

both ways, but not last night, and not on Saturday, either."

I nodded. There was no humor in the smile I gave him, just promise.

"Have a good day, Mr. Carriere."

"You too, Mr. Starke, and take care, you hear?"

I walked east from the docks, across a small bridge and out onto the third fairway. From where I was standing, the rear of the Mount was maybe a quarter mile away, certainly less than five hundred yards. I walked back to the bridge, a humpy wooden structure that joined the mainland to the marina. I stood for a moment, my hands on the rail, looking both ways, back at the *Gabby II* and then at the Mount, high on the rise to the east. *It's easily doable. But it's really exposed. Surely someone would have seen him. Hmmm, but maybe not. And if they did, they probably wouldn't have taken any notice....*

"I didn't do it, Mr. Starke."

I looked around. I hadn't heard him following me, and he was about to step onto the bridge.

He joined me at the rail. "Yes, I could have easily made it up there, but I didn't. Not either time. I loved Gabby, and I didn't give a flying monkey for Alicia. I didn't kill either of them."

There was something in his voice that made me inclined to believe him.

232

"No. I don't believe you did. Do you have any idea who might have?"

He shook his head. "No. I wasn't that tight with the family. Like I said on the boat, I'm not exactly the kind of person any of them wanted her to marry, so I pretty much kept myself to myself. They're a weird bunch though, especially Evander. If I had to choose, he would be the one."

"What about the butler, Moore?"

"What about him?"

"Alicia Margolis accused him of trying to rape her. She said you stopped him. True?"

"Jeez, that woman. No. In fact, I think that the opposite is probably true. I walked into the living room just as he pushed her away. She flew at him, claws first. I... restrained her."

I nodded. "Was Gabrielle having an affair with Moore?"

His eyes narrowed. He looked troubled. "Perhaps she was. I don't know." And with that he left and walked back to the *Gabby II*. I stood for a moment, watching him go, thinking, and then I walked west along the dock, searching for Kate and admiring the boats along the way. I wondered what kind of a person would want to invest so much in such a luxury, and then it hit me.

I was.

Yeah. I could do that, so long as I had someone to sail it for me.

I found Kate sitting outside a small shack sipping on the Calypso Key version of a smoothie. I ordered one for myself, with a splash of rum in it—perfect—and a small bowl of conch salad, and sat down beside her.

"So, what did you find out?" I asked her.

"Not much. No one claims to have seen him, that day or this, and there he is, large as life." She waved her straw in the general direction of the *Gabby II.* I looked around and saw the tiny figure back up on the flying bridge. He had his hands on the rail and was obviously watching us, although from that distance how he could see much was beyond me.

"They're not saying he wasn't here, just that they don't remember seeing him."

"He told me they were a pretty tight bunch, that you wouldn't get much out of them. One thing I do know is that it wouldn't have been difficult for him to make it across the golf course to the house, even at night, but I don't think he did."

"How come? That second sight of yours kicking in again?"

"Something like that, but no; I really think he loved Gabrielle. I don't think he would have harmed her, and that, by default, means he didn't do the other one either. He also told me Moore didn't try to rape Alicia."

"I figured," she said.

"I asked him if he thought Gabrielle was having an affair with Moore. He said he didn't know, but that it was possible. The question seemed to upset him. Not surprising, I suppose."

234

She nodded. I looked at my watch. It was almost one o'clock.

"Let's go," I said. "I'd like to spend some time with Amanda this afternoon."

"How's that going?" she asked as we walked to the car.

I looked sideways at her. "Me and Amanda? Fine. Why do you ask?"

"Oh, I was just wondering. Never in a million years would I have believed you'd ever settle down... and, now don't take this the wrong way, certainly not with Amanda. You and she have quite a history."

"That thing she did to me on TV, you mean?"

She nodded.

"I got over that a long time ago. You're right though; who would have thought it? So, seeing as we're on the subject; how about you and Bob?"

She took her time answering, then, "It's good, I suppose. He hasn't said so, but I know he loves me. Do I love him though? That's the question."

"Well. Do you?"

"It's only been a few weeks. I could do a whole lot worse, I guess. He's a big old bear, but soft as a kitten. He can kill a man without a second thought, yet I've seen him scooping bugs out of the pool. I could definitely do worse."

"You sure could," I said.

She smiled at me. "You're so biased. He's like a brother to… you…. Harry, I'm so sorry. That was so thoughtless of me."

"Henry, you mean? Nah. We can't hide that away as if it never happened. It did. I'll live with it. But back to you and Bob. I hope you two can make it work."

"Me too," she said, a little wistfully. "Me too. You and Amanda seem happy together. I could really do with some of that."

Chapter 27

The sun rose over the ocean, the herald of another beautiful day. Me? Once again, I hadn't slept a whole lot. Amanda? She'd slept like a dead dog. As usual.

I was out early. I went for a run along the beach well before daylight. I arrived back at the cottage to find her still asleep. I took a long, hot shower—that's the place I get most of my bright ideas, but this time nothing came, and it bothered me. No, the whole scenario bothered me, and I couldn't put my finger on why.

I dried myself off, made coffee—two cups—and went into the bedroom; she was just beginning to stir.

I handed her a cup and watched as she lifted it to her lips. There were many things I loved about Amanda, and the show she always made of that first cup of coffee was one of them.

"Okay," she said, looking up at me through her eyelashes. "What's on your mind? There's something, I can tell."

"I'd like some time alone today, to think. Do you mind?"

"It's the case, right?"

I nodded.

"Of course not. Why would I?"

"Damn it, Amanda. This is supposed to be our honeymoon."

"I know that, silly goose, but you need to do this. You'll figure it out. You always do. When it's done, though, I want you all to myself. Deal?"

"Deal."

When we finally made it out to breakfast, I was back where I had been in the shower: my brain was a total wipeout, and I soon became lost in a whirl of thoughts that kept spinning back and forth through my head. Three cups of Dark Italian Roast later, with a fourth in my hands, I headed back to the cottage, leaving the others to enjoy the morning. The cottage had its own private patio with a table, chairs, and a couple of loungers, and that's where I settled in.

I opened my laptop, set my phone to vibrate, laid my iPad down beside the laptop, and my digital recorder next to that. Then I sucked down what was left of the coffee, lay down on one of the loungers, and stared up at the slowly spinning fan. I closed my eyes, took a deep breath, turned my brain loose, and let the movie run. But a movie it surely wasn't. What it was, was a disjointed jumble of bits and pieces of scenes and conversations that made no sense at all, but hidden somewhere among them, I had a feeling, lay the answers I was looking for.

It must have been a couple of hours later when something nudged my subconscious. I don't know if I'd dozed off and had been dreaming or what, but I knew it was worth checking out. I sat up and grabbed the recorder from the table, turned it on at the beginning, and let it run. I flipped the lock screen on my iPad and opened my notes, and then followed along as the recorder chirped, comparing my notes to the conversations and interviews. By the time I found it, I'd played the recordings through three times, fast-forwarding, backtracking, playing sections over and over....

By the time I was done, it was after five and I was starving; I was also one happy investigator.

"Well, did you figure it out?" Amanda asked when I found her.

"I think so. I still need something... but I'm not entirely sure what."

It was almost nine thirty that evening when my iPhone vibrated on the glass tabletop. I was out on the patio, by myself. Amanda was taking a bath and I was alone with my Scottish friend, Mr. Laphroaig. It was Daisy Patel calling.

"Hey, Daisy," I answered. "What's up?"

"I pulled in a couple of favors and got the DNA analysis on the blood spot rushed. I just got the results back. You're not going to be happy. It's degraded—by the solvents used to clean the carpet, I have no doubt. The only thing I can tell you for sure is that it's not Gabrielle's. Other than that... nothing. Sorry."

239

"Damn," I said under my breath. "Anything else?'

"Not much. Other than the shards of broken milk glass there's some debris, fibers, and hairs from the carpet. And a smudge on the base of the wine glass that wasn't enough to be of any use. But there was a partial print on the condom wrapper. I'll send it to you."

"Hmmm. Okay, thanks, Daisy. The print on the wrapper will belong to Carriere, but we'll check to make sure. Thanks for the call, and for your extra effort. I really appreciate it."

"No problem, Harry. Good luck."

Slowly, I laid the phone back down on the tabletop and stared at it. It seemed to stare back at me, mocking me. *Damn, damn, damn. What the hell do I do now?*

Then I remembered what Amanda had said to me on the beach. What was it she'd called me? The king of deception and trickery. *Oh that's not true. Not true at all.... Hmmm. Okay, I think I know who did it, but how the hell do I prove it? What exactly do I have? Damn, without that DNA, I have nothing....*

For another hour I sat there by myself, nursing one Laphroaig after another. I don't know whether it was the calming effect of one of Scotland's finest malt whiskeys, or the fact that it cleared my head—yeah that's what I said, cleared my head. Whatever. When I finally felt Amanda's hands on my shoulders, I had the bare bones of a plan. Would it work? Hell, who knew? What I did know was that if it didn't, the killer was going to get away with it.

Jeez. It has to work. I don't have anything else.

"Come on, Harry. It's getting late. Come to bed."

I don't know how anyone could resist such a request, especially coming from her, but I did. I wasn't quite ready yet.

"Not yet. I need to run something by you. Sit down. I'll order you a drink."

"Like this?" She walked around in front of me, and when I looked up at her I almost choked on my Laphroaig.

She stood in front of me, feet apart, her hands on her hips, smiling down at me.

Amanda is five foot nine and stunningly beautiful. She has a pair of legs that seem to go on forever. That night she was wearing three-inch heels and an almost sheer, black floral lace chemise and a matching thong.

Oh. My. God.

"Um, no… go put on a robe or something and then come back, but don't you dare take that thing off. I want to do that."

She pouted, swished her hips from side to side. "You sure?"

"Positive. On both counts. Now for God's sake get outa here before I crack. I need to do this. I'll order you a glass of wine. I need to talk."

She was gone for only a couple of minutes, but before she could sit down, I took her hand. "Show me."

She stood in front of me, cocked one knee up, and opened the resort robe wide. Again, the breath was sucked out of me. Under the robe, the damned outfit seemed even more erotic, if that were possible.

I sat there and stared at her, and I stared at her, and I....

"Oh for Pete's sake, Harry," Amanda laughed, "that's enough." And she wrapped herself up again, sat down beside me, took my hand, and leaned in and kissed me. And when I say she kissed me, she really went for it.

"Now then," she said, leaning back in her seat. "That was just a little taste of what's for dessert."

"What, no cream? Ow, that hurt." She'd slapped my wounded arm.

"Oh, Harry. I'm sorry. I keep forgetting. Here, let me kiss it better." And she did.

The waiter came with the wine just as she let me go.

"Would like me to pour, sir?"

"Yes, please," I said, laughing up at him. "The wine is just for the lady."

"Of course," he said as he handed her the glass.

She took it from him, sipped, nodded, and placed it on the table.

"Will there be anything else?" the waiter asked.

"Not right now, but check back in ten minutes or so, if you don't mind."

He nodded and left.

"So," she said. "What did you want to talk to me about?"

"I have a plan I'd like to run by you...."

"Wouldn't it be better if you ran it by Kate?"

"It probably would, but she doesn't look like you.... No! Not again." I reared away from her as she raised her hand.

"Big baby. I was just reaching for my drink." And she was.

For the next twenty minutes or so, we tossed my idea back and forth, back and forth. I refined it, teased it, tweaked it, until I was sure I could pull it off, and then I could stand it no longer. I stood up, took her hand, and led her like a sulky little brat back into the cottage, and then the bedroom, and finished the evening with... well. Use your imagination.

Chapter 28

That next morning I called Tommy Quinn and asked him to come on over from St. Thomas. He said that he would, but also that it would be a while before he could get there because he had to come by boat; the helicopter was being serviced.

In the meantime, I met Kate and Bob for breakfast and outlined my plan.

"Oh my God," Kate said. "You're going to do the Inspector Clouseau thing, gather them all together and do the big reveal?"

Bob grinned. "That should be a laugh."

"Well, I need to flush the killer out," I said. "I know who it is, or at least I think I do, but I can't prove it."

"What happens if he doesn't freak?" Kate asked.

"Nothing. I'm screwed, and he walks. But I don't think that will happen."

"So who is it?" Bob asked.

Now it was my turn to grin. "If I tell you, it'll spoil my Clouseau act. You'll just have to wait and see."

"Damn, Harry. You've been watching too many old movies."

Next I called Leo Martan and told him that we would like to meet with everyone in the living room. We set the appointment for noon.

Once Tommy arrived, we drove up to the Mount together, and with a couple of exceptions, which didn't matter, they were all there waiting for us, and they weren't happy. Leo Jr. was angry as hell. He claimed he'd had to miss an important appointment to be there. Evan looked like he might be on something, and probably was. Georgina, his girlfriend, was drumming her fingers on the table. The Collinses were seated together, holding hands. Jeffery Margolis was standing by the fireplace; his face as white as a sheet. Moore stood stoically beside the door, his hands clasped behind his back, looking for all the world like someone who was ready to make a run for it should the need arise. Vivien, Sebastian, and the gardener were not present. No one looked at ease.

I made a point of shaking everyone's hand and thanking them for their time and patience and for attending. Telling them thank you was an attempt to mollify them; shaking their hands was not.

Until then, I'd had a good idea who the killer was, but wasn't absolutely sure; by the time the round of handshakes was done, I was.

I stood with my back to the window, laid my iPad on the table in front of me, and looked around the room.

And then I began.

"I'm not going to waste a lot of time handing out a bunch of theories—who did what to whom and when. I'm not Colombo, but I do know that one of you killed both Gabrielle and Alicia. You all had motives. Several of you had very strong motives, money being the most obvious. Most of you had opportunity. All of you had the means."

I looked at them. There was not a sound to be heard. No one did so much as blink.

"You know who you are," I said. "And so do I. I know because by killing Alicia you made a huge mistake." I paused. There was no reaction.

"Like most people who think they're smart enough to get away with murder, you went a step too far; you tried to divert attention away from yourself by killing a suspect and then trying to make it look like she committed suicide. The idea being of course that she killed herself because she either thought she was about to be exposed, or because she couldn't live with herself after killing Gabrielle.

"In this case, however, the ploy had the opposite effect. In fact it was overkill. First, it removed Alicia from the list of suspects, and second... it actually drew attention to you, the real killer."

I was watching Leo Jr. intently as I said it, and I enjoyed watched him squirm, and I smiled to myself.

"Something had been bothering me for days," I continued. "I knew I was missing something, something about Gabrielle's murder, but it wasn't until I went back over the recorded interviews that I finally figured it out, and when I did, I knew who the murderer was."

Well, I thought I did.

"The problem was that I couldn't prove it. I had no physical evidence. And then the killer helped me out by killing Alicia." I paused as I looked at each of them in turn, then turned my attention back to Leo Jr., and continued.

"You see, it's a well-known tenet in law enforcement that every perpetrator of a crime either leaves something at the scene, or takes something away. This case is no different. The killer, in both cases, left something behind.

"In Gabrielle's case, it was a single spot of blood. We found it in the carpet in Gabrielle's room. The angle of the cut on her head indicated a right-handed blow. The blow itself was not hard enough to kill her, but it was hard enough to break the weapon. We know that weapon was a bottle made of milk glass. We know because we found several shards in the pile of the carpet. That being so, we figured it was highly likely the blood spot came from a cut on the killer's right hand…. True, it could have been Gabrielle's, fallen from

247

the cut on her forehead, but most likely it was the killer's. We didn't know for sure until we got the results of the DNA tests back. Those came in last night. The blood did indeed belong to her killer." *And that's no lie,* I thought. *It didn't belong to Gabrielle, so....*

"In Alicia's case it was a partial fingerprint that the killer left on the base of a glass in the room." *Not exactly a lie, but it was just a smudge, and useless.*

"She, Alicia, was drugged, by the way. Ketamine...."

As I said that last bit I switched my attention from Leo and looked straight at Lucy Martan, and I watched as the color drained from her face.

"That's a nasty cut you have in the web of your right hand, Lucy," I said quietly, watching her eyes.

She covered her right hand with her left, staring at me through eyes that had narrowed into slits of hate. Her lips were clamped shut in a tight, thin line.

"Horses," I said. "They're your forte, right? And ketamine is a horse tranquilizer, often used as a date-rape drug. Hmmm. But there's more, isn't there, Lucy? Would you like to tell me how you knew Gabrielle had been hit with a bottle before any of us did?"

"What are you talking about? I didn't know that...."

"Yes you did. Listen to this. It's part of your interview on Sunday morning." I withdrew the recorder from my pants pocket and flipped the switch.

"So she was screwing Jeff for sure, and maybe Moore, the butler, and probably Jackson and Michael too? So someone lost their temper and hit her over the head with a bottle? Does that surprise *you, for God's sake?"*

For a moment she just sat there, staring at the recorder in my hand. And then, without warning, she exploded. She uttered an ear-piercing scream, leaped to her feet, and threw herself at me across the table, her hands curled into talons, her nails into claws.

I shouldn't have been, but I was taken completely by surprise. Only by reflex and instinct was I able to avoid the fingers aimed at my eyes. I managed to knock those aside, but the talons became fists and she began to pummel me for all she was worth. The edge of her fist came down with all the force she could muster on my injured arm, right on the wound. White-hot pain speared up my arm all the way to the back of my eyes. I swear I almost blacked out.

Fortunately, help was at hand in the form of Victor Moore. He leapt over the table, grabbed her around the waist, and lugged her out through the French doors onto the patio, kicking and screaming.

As the throbbing pain in my arm slowly began to subside, I sat down and watched as Tommy Quinn cuffed her: not an easy job. The woman was strong, and she'd totally lost it. She fought, she screamed, she scratched, she bit, but finally he and Moore got her under control, and she sat under an umbrella, hands behind her back, head down, sobbing.

"Why?" Leo Martan Sr. asked as he walked us back to the car. "Why did she do it?"

"Money," I replied. "It's almost always about money. Your son's broke. He wouldn't ask you for help, so she decided to help herself. She knew about Gabrielle's inheritance and the dispersal clause should anything happen to Gabrielle. She knew the money would come to her husband, so she killed her. Alicia was, as I said, her big mistake. She thought she could divert attention away from herself. The funny thing is, at that time she, Lucy, wasn't even a suspect; Alicia was. Like you, I figured it was either Alicia or your wife—your secret is safe with me, by the way," I said, grinning at him.

He gave me a wry smile in return. "What will happen to her?" he asked.

Oh boy. This was the part I hadn't been looking forward to. I looked at him, shook my head, looked down.

"I'm not sure. Oh, she did it all right; she lost it back there—but she admitted nothing." I shook my head. "I hate to say it, but without a confession, she'll probably walk."

"She won't be convicted?" He was incredulous.

"If she gets herself a good lawyer, I very much doubt it. Look, you asked me to find out who killed your daughter, and I did. We know she did it, but what little proof we have is circumstantial. The only real piece of evidence we have is that recording, and even that's dubious. What she said about the bottle, that's circumstantial too. A good lawyer will suggest that her choice of words, "the bottle"—we never found it, by the way—was purely coincidental, and that she could just as easily have said hammer, candlestick, or whatever. Oh, Tommy Quinn knows she did it. We all do, and he'll grill her, try to get a confession. But if I know my perps, when she calms down, she'll get wise. If she does, it's not going to happen. She'll lawyer up, and that'll be the end of it." I shrugged and shook my head.

"If he does manage to get a confession, she'll go to jail. If not…. Well, she'll probably walk out of there within forty-eight hours and come on home."

"But what about the DNA, the fingerprint on the glass?"

I smiled at him. I didn't have the heart to tell him. "We'll see," I said. "We'll see."

We reached car and I turned to shake his hand. It was then that I saw Victor Moore standing at the top of the steps, watching us. He looked at me, narrowed his eyes, and nodded, slowly. I got the message. He knew what I knew... and then I remembered his promise.

Chapter 29

It was almost three o'clock when Kate, Bob, and I returned to the resort. I spent the afternoon with Amanda; she iced my throbbing arm. I took more ibuprofen, and we sat together by the pool.

"So you think she'll get away with it, then?"

"Yup. That's the problem when you have to fall back on deception to get the job done."

"Deception?"

"Yeah, your idea, right?"

She stared at me.

"Don't worry. It was a good one. If I hadn't resorted to fudging the truth a little, old man Martan would still be wondering who killed his kid and stepdaughter."

"Okay, that's enough. So what are we going to do with the rest of our honeymoon? We only have four days left."

I smiled slyly at her. "What do you think?"

"Apart from that, dumbass."

"Oh, dumbass is it? I get it. Now you've gotten your hooks into me I get to see the real you, is that it?"

"No. I love you, Harry."

253

"And I love you too, and I have a surprise for you, but I'll tell you about it later. Now let's go swimming in the ocean, but this time...."

"Oh don't worry," she said, smiling. "I'll look after you."

It was almost ten o'clock that evening when I made my big announcement. Dinner was finished, but everyone was still there, and it seemed as good a time as any.

I stood up and tapped my glass with a dessert spoon to get their attention. "Dad. Everyone," I said. "Since we're all here together, I just wanted to let you guys know something." I squeezed Amanda's hand. "You too, sweetheart." She looked up at me, her eyes wide.

"When this is vacation is over, Amanda and I won't be going back with you." There was a collective gasp, including one from Amanda, and she squeezed my hand hard.

"It's not what you think. We're just going to stay here for a while, through Christmas and the new year. I need a break in the worst way, and...." I looked down at Amanda. "And I need to spend some time with Amanda as far away from the real world as we can get. I need to give my arm a chance to heal properly. I need to grieve for Henry, and I need to rest, boy do I ever need to rest. I had a chat with Captain Walker and I've chartered the *Lady May* until January 6. We'll fly back on the seventh. We'll leave on an extended cruise when you fly home. We'll sail the islands and then hit the new year with a new outlook on life, and maybe something a little more." I squeezed her hand and glanced at her; her eyes were glistening.

"Good for you, son," August said. "It's about damned time."

"What about the agency?" Jacque asked.

"It's yours and Bob's until I get back. You can handle things between you. You've both been around me long enough to know what I would do in any given situation. If you don't, I don't care. You'll just have to manage somehow. Oh, and Kate. I'm going to ask you one more time…. Come and work for me. You and Bob get along great. You'd make a fine team and… well, you might as well know, all of you. I am coming back to run the business, but not like before. I'm going to hand off some of the responsibilities, to you Jacque, Bob, and you, Kate, if you'll accept my offer."

But Kate was shaking her head. "I can't do it, Harry. I'm a cop. Always will be. Besides, what would you do without me on the inside?"

"Damn it," Bob growled.

"Oh well," I said. "It was worth a shot."

"And—" she was laughing now "—there's no way I could spend my working days in the company of that big lug. The nights are more than enough for me."

I couldn't help it. I put back my head and laughed.

"Is that so?" Bob asked, as he grabbed her and laid a kiss on her that Tom Cruise would have been proud of.

They do make a damn fine couple, don't they?

And then everyone was laughing and talking and leaning over their chairs like children; the volume of conversation in the room shot up. August got up out of his seat and came around the table. I turned to meet him. He wrapped his arms around me and whispered, "I love you, son."

I knew he did, but I think that might have been the first time he'd ever come right out and said it.

"I love you too, Dad."

I was still holding Amanda's hand, and I could feel her trembling. She was crying when I looked down at her. Tears ran freely down her cheeks. I sat down again and pulled her to me.

"It's okay, my love," I said. "We'll have a wonderful time."

"I know we will," she whispered. I could hear in her voice that she was smiling. "I know we will."

Thank you.

Thank you for taking the time to read *Calypso*. If you enjoyed it, please consider telling your friends and posting a short review on Amazon (just a sentence will do). Word of mouth is an author's best friend, and much appreciated. Thank you. —Blair Howard.

Reviews are so very important. I don't have the backing of a major New York publisher, and I can't afford take out ads in the newspapers or on TV, but you can help get the word out.

To those many of my readers who have already posted reviews to this and my other novels, thank you for your past and continued support.

If you have comments or questions, you can contact me by e-mail at blair@blairhoward.com, and you can visit my website http://www.blairhoward.com.

This story was Book 8 in the Harry Starke series. If you haven't already read them, you may also enjoy reading the other Harry Starke novels. They are all stand-alone stories: no cliffhangers.

Harry Starke—Book 1

It's almost midnight, bitterly cold, snowing, when a beautiful young girl, Tabitha Willard, throws herself off the Walnut Street Bridge into the icy waters of the Tennessee. Harry Starke is there, on the bridge. Wrong time, wrong place? Maybe. He tries, but is unable to stop her. Thus begins a series of events and an investigation that involves a local United States congressman, a senior lady senator from Boston, a local crime boss, several very nasty individuals, sex, extortion, high finance, corruption, and three murders. Harry has to work his way through a web of deceit and corruption until finally.... Well, as always, there's a twist in the tale. Several, in fact.

You can grab your copy here:

Amazon U.S. http://amzn.to/1K8zCrl

Amazon U.K. http://amzn.to/1RUx5XW

If you're a Kindle Unlimited member, you can read it for free.

Two for the Money—Harry Starke Book 2

Who Killed Tom Sattler? Who stole $350 million from New Vision Strategic Investments?

It's up to Harry Starke to figure it out.

The call came on a Tuesday evening in the middle of August at around nine thirty. It was from an old school friend that Harry Starke hadn't heard from in almost five years, and he hadn't thought about him in almost as long. Tom Sattler wanted to meet with Harry urgently, and it wouldn't wait until morning. When Harry arrived at Sattler's luxury home less than an hour later, he found him dead, lying in a pool of blood, a single gunshot wound to the head, and .22 revolver lying close to his hand.

Suicide? If he was going to do that, why the hell did he call Harry?

The search for an answer to that question starts Harry on a wide-ranging investigation that involves murder, corruption, organized crime, and deception.

You can grab your copy here:

Amazon U.S. and here's the actual link: http://amzn.to/1MRsdmo

Amazon U.K. or http://amzn.to/1KlQk6n

As always, if you're a Kindle Unlimited member, you can read it for free.

Hill House—Harry Starke Book 3

For more than ten years, she lay beneath the floorboards of Hill House. For more than ten years, she waited. Who was she? Who put her there? Why? Harry Starke vows to find the answers to those questions, but to do so he must embark upon an investigation that will put him and those close to him in deadly danger, take him deep into the underground city, the Dark Web, murder, organized crime, prostitution, and human trafficking. One by one, he peels back the layers, and with each one, he sinks a little deeper into the morass, the seamy underbelly of a world few know of, and even fewer want to be a part of. Hill

House has many doors. None of them lead anywhere but into darkness and despair.

You can grab your copy here:

Amazon U.S. http://amzn.to/1P7KFYU

Amazon U.K. http://amzn.to/1ZbMqY3

If you're a Kindle Unlimited member, you can read it for free.

Checkmate—Harry Starke Book 4

They found Angela Hartwell lying in the shallow waters beside the golf course. There was not a mark on her, yet she was dead, strangled. How could that be?

Once again, it's up to Harry Starke to find out. The investigation takes him into a world he's very familiar with, a world of affluence, privilege and… corruption.

To solve the mystery, he must deal with three murders, a beautiful used car dealer, her lovely twin sisters, and a crooked banker. Not to mention Burke and Hare, two crazy repo men who will stop at nothing to protect their employer's interests. There's also the matter of an ingenious, sadistic killer. But nothing is ever quite what it seems….

You can grab your copy of *Checkmate* here:

Amazon U.S. http://amzn.to/1SQhf4q

Amazon U.K. http://amzn.to/20AVnc7

If you're a Kindle Unlimited member, you can read it for free.

GONE – Harry Starke Book 5

Emily Johnston is gone. She's been gone for more than a week. She's also the daughter of Harry Starke's one-time boss and nemesis, Chattanooga Police Chief Wesley Johnston. Harry and Chief Johnston haven't seen eye-to-eye in a long time, but when Johnston needs help, he knows there's only one man he can turn to.

But Johnston's jurisdiction ends at the city limits, and when Emily's body is discovered in a remote part of the county, Harry has to deal with the imperious sheriff, Israel Hands, and two incompetent county detectives. So begins an investigation that will take Harry on a wild ride across Signal Mountain, a case that will include a second murder, two cold cases, sex, alternative lifestyles, and deadly danger for Harry and his friends, until... well, as always, there's a twist in the tale.

You can grab your copy here:
Amazon U.S. http://amzn.to/2aePpwG
Amazon U.K. http://amzn.to/29PsLJS

If you're a Kindle Unlimited member, you can read it for free.

Family Matters – Harry Starke Book 6

Harry Starke loves a cold case, but this one is really cold—more than a hundred years cold.

Family Matters is a whimsical tale, a flight of fancy. It takes place on the lonely coast of Maine, where Amanda, a true believer in the paranormal, has inherited—you guessed it—a haunted house. Or at least that's what the rumors say.

It all begins when Amanda inherits the house, substantial assets, and a large sum of money from her grandmother. The windfall comes with a request to look into the disappearance of Elizabeth, Amanda's great-great-grandmother, more than a hundred years ago.

Harry, a skeptic, a down-to-earth investigator who believes only in the facts, has a tough time dealing with Amanda's... fantasies? We all know that the imagination can play tricks on a susceptible mind, especially when that mind is under stress. But is it just their imaginations? Could it be something more?

You'll have to be the judge.

You can grab your copy here:

Amazon U.S. http://amzn.to/1VgRv1R

Amazon U.K. http://amzn.to/23ulMM6

If you're a Kindle Unlimited member, you can read it for free.

Retribution - Harry Starke Book 7

Shadows from the past. A brutal murder. This time it's personal.

It takes only one phone call to turn Harry Starke into a monster. It begins when Harry's kid brother is brutally murdered, his body thrown into the murky waters of the Tennessee River. That alone would be enough to set Harry on the warpath, but less than twenty-four hours after the body is found, Harry finds out there's a bounty on his head, too. $25,000. His answer? Strike first and strike hard. And so it begins. Harry and his army of three must go up against old enemies, but they face almost insurmountable odds when they go looking for… retribution.

You can grab your copy here:

Amazon U.S. http://amzn.to/2aWxMAH

Amazon U.K. http://amzn.to/2b8MBo1

If you're a Kindle Unlimited member, you can read it for free.

Printed in the USA
CPSIA information can be obtained
at www.ICGtesting.com
LVHW012310181223
766854LV00053B/1460

9 781539 190059